CHABOUTÉ

TO BUILD A FIRE

BASED ON JACK LONDON'S CLASSIC STORY

TRANSLATION BY LAURA WATERS

GALLERY 13

New York   London   Toronto   Sydney   New Delhi

Gallery 13
An Imprint of Simon & Schuster, Inc.
1230 Avenue of the Americas
New York, NY 10020

Originally published in France by Editions Glénat, S.A. as *Construire un Feu*

English language translation copyright © 2018 by Simon & Schuster, Inc.
English language translation performed by Laura Waters.

First Gallery 13 trade paperback edition October 2018

GALLERY 13 and colophon are trademarks of Simon & Schuster, Inc.

For information about special discounts for bulk purchases, please contact Simon & Schuster Special Sales at 1-866-506-1949 or business@simonandschuster.com.

The Simon & Schuster Speakers Bureau can bring authors to your live event. For more information or to book an event contact the Simon & Schuster Speakers Bureau at 1-866-248-3049 or visit our website at www.simonspeakers.com.

Manufactured in the United States of America

10 9 8 7 6 5 4 3 2 1

Library of Congress Cataloging-in-Publication Data is available.

ISBN 978-1-9821-0082-7
ISBN 978-1-9821-0083-4 (ebook)

IN 1896, RICH GOLD-BEARING DEPOSITS WERE DISCOVERED IN THE KLONDIKE REGION OF NORTHERN CANADA. ALL OVER AMERICA, THIS NEWS SPREAD LIKE WILDFIRE.

IN THE MIDDLE OF AN ECONOMIC CRISIS, GOLD FEVER ATTRACTED THOUSANDS OF AMATEUR ADVENTURERS TOWARD THE SAVAGE AND UNEXPLORED LANDS OF THE GREAT NORTH.

CLOSE TO A HUNDRED THOUSAND AMERICANS FASHIONED THEMSELVES AS PROSPECTORS AND SPED IN A FRENZY TOWARD THESE TERRITORIES AND THEIR FABLED FIELDS OF GOLD.

THE FIRST OF THE DIFFICULTIES THESE EXPLORERS ENCOUNTERED WAS GETTING TO THE KLONDIKE WHEN METHODS OF COMMUNICATION WERE PRACTICALLY NONEXISTENT.

RUDIMENTARY PATHS ALLOWED ACCESS TO CANADA FROM THE ALASKAN COAST THROUGH THE MOUNTAINS . . . EACH CONTENDER FOR FORTUNE HAD TO BRING WITH HIM ALL THE ITEMS NECESSARY TO SURVIVE FOR A YEAR, WHICH COMPRISED SIX TO NINE HUNDRED POUNDS OF FOOD AND TOOLS: IN TOTAL CLOSE TO A TON OF EQUIPMENT.

THOUSANDS OF MEN, QUESTING FOR FORTUNE OR ADVENTURE, LOST THEMSELVES AND PERISHED IN THIS DESERT OF SNOW AND ICE.

FREQUENTLY INEXPERIENCED AND POORLY EQUIPPED, THEY WERE FORCED TO CONFRONT A HOSTILE NATURAL LANDSCAPE, VANQUISH ISOLATION, HUNGER, SCURVY, AND ABOVE ALL FACE AN ENEMY TERRIBLE AND WITHOUT PITY . . .

THE COLD . . .

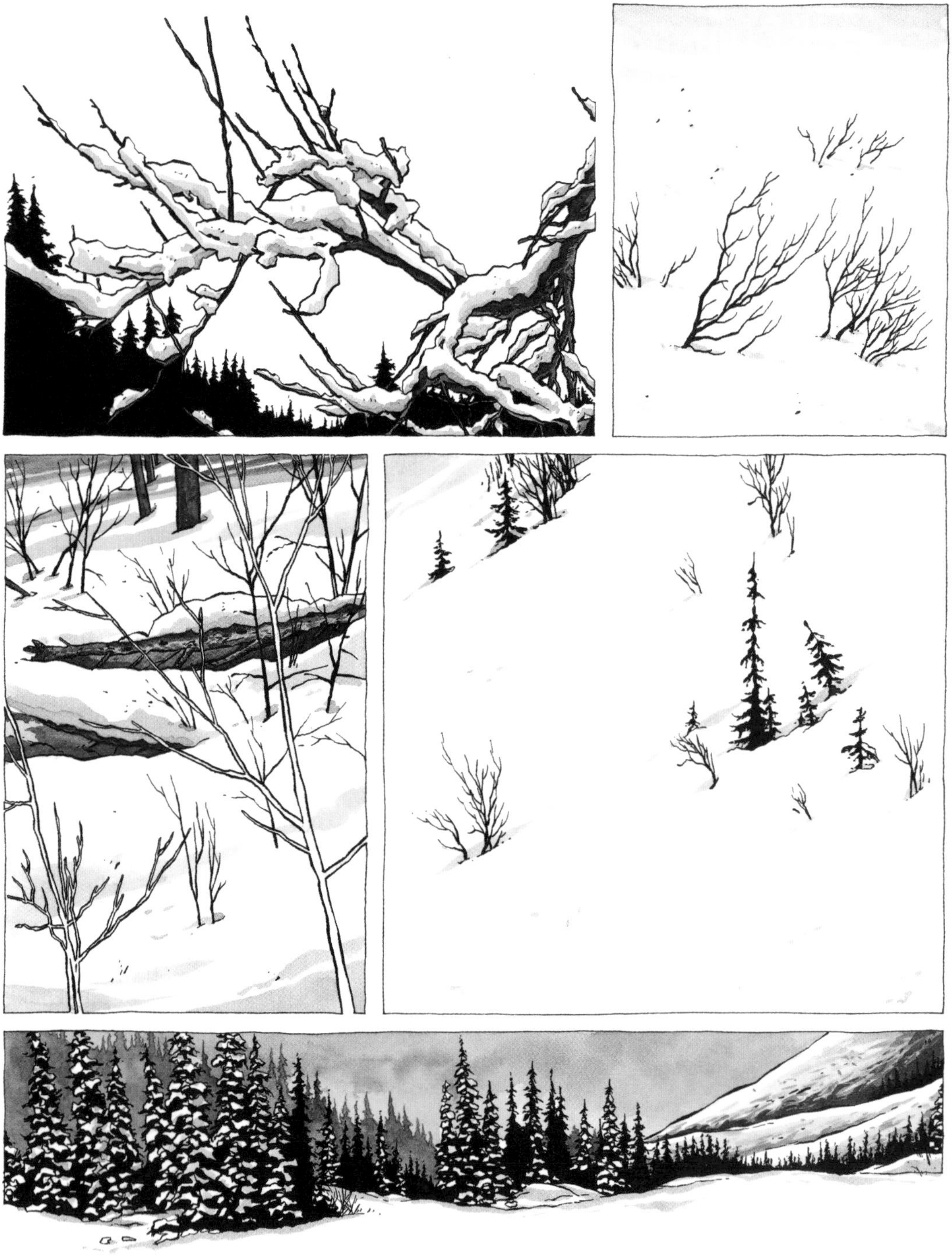

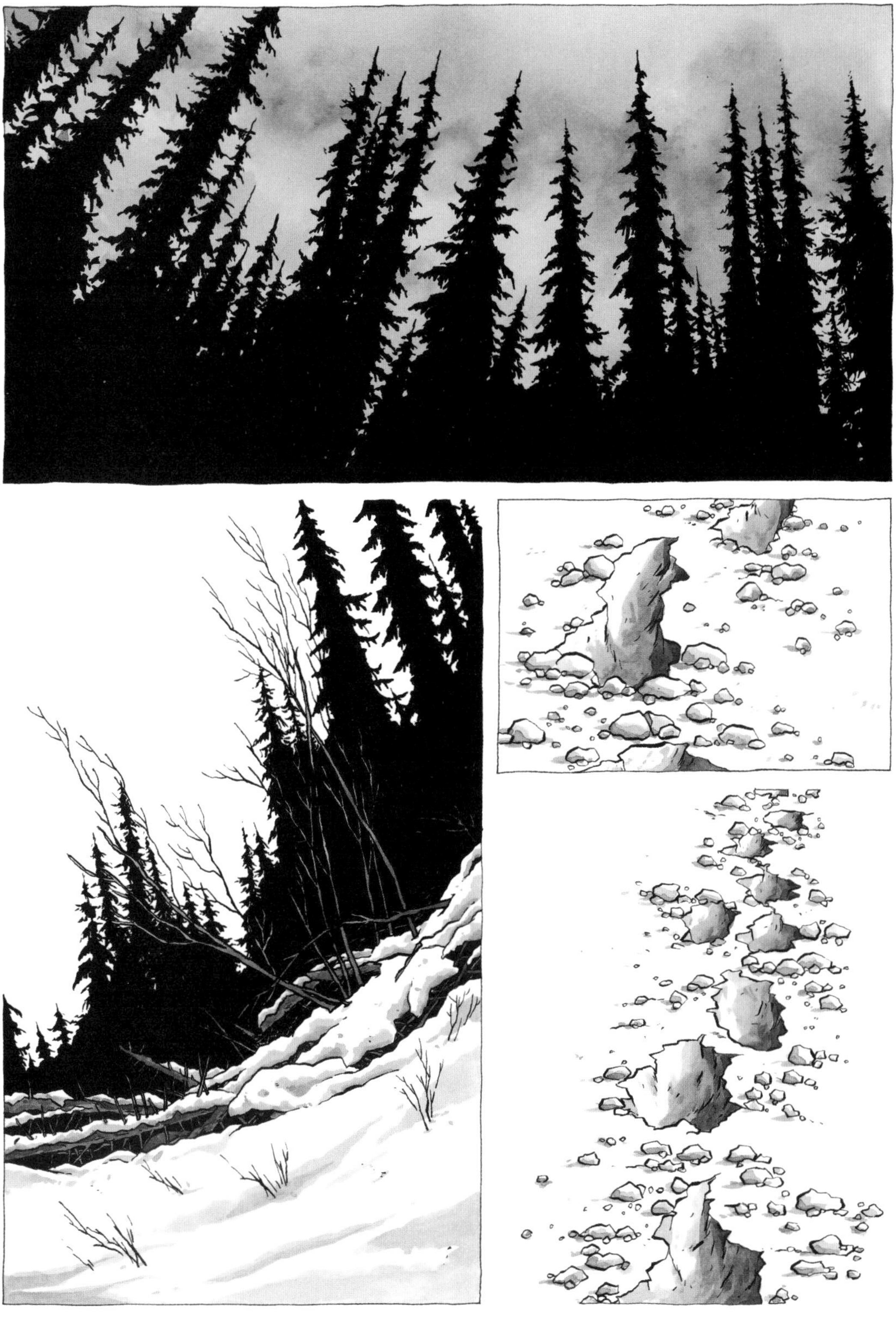

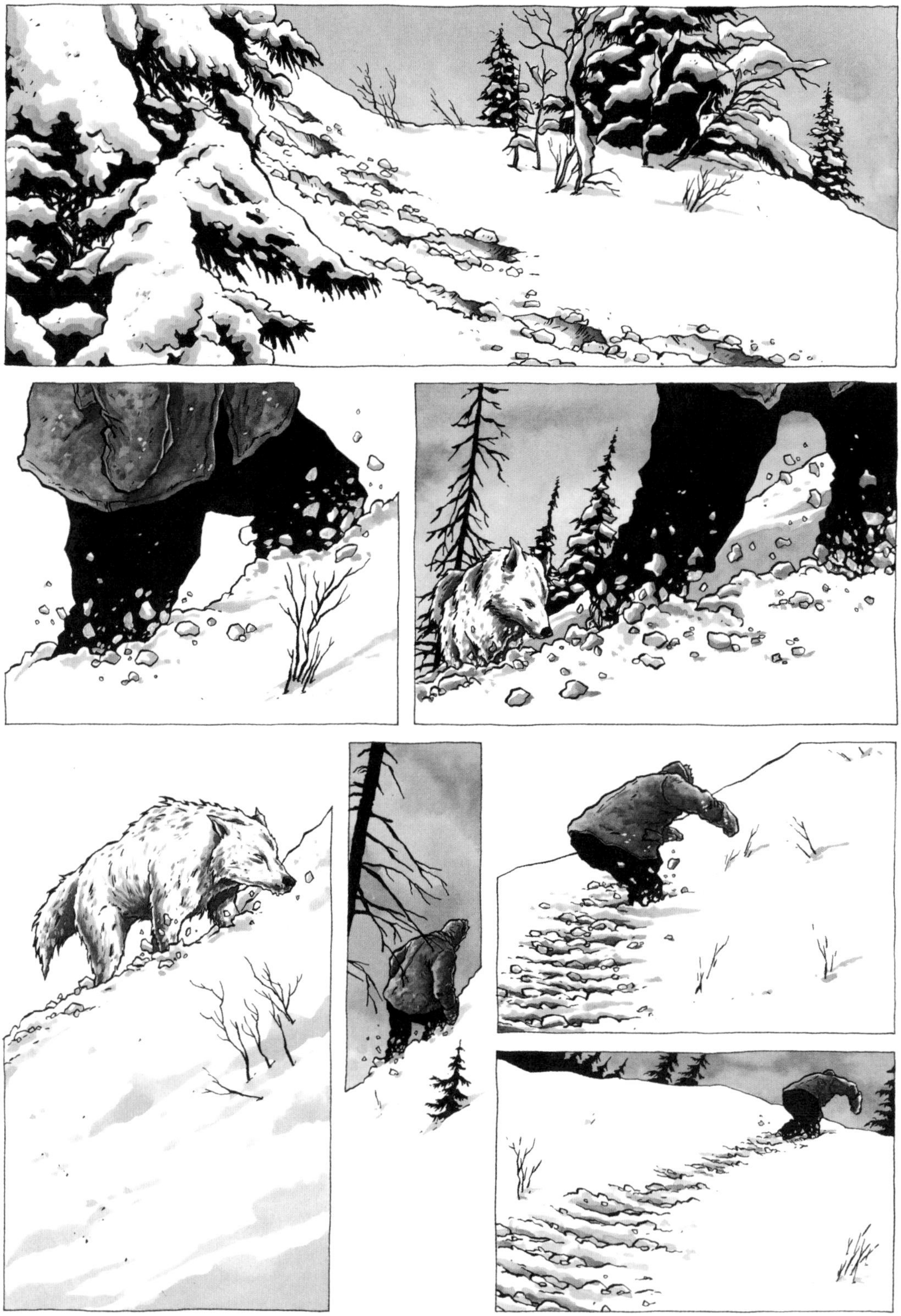

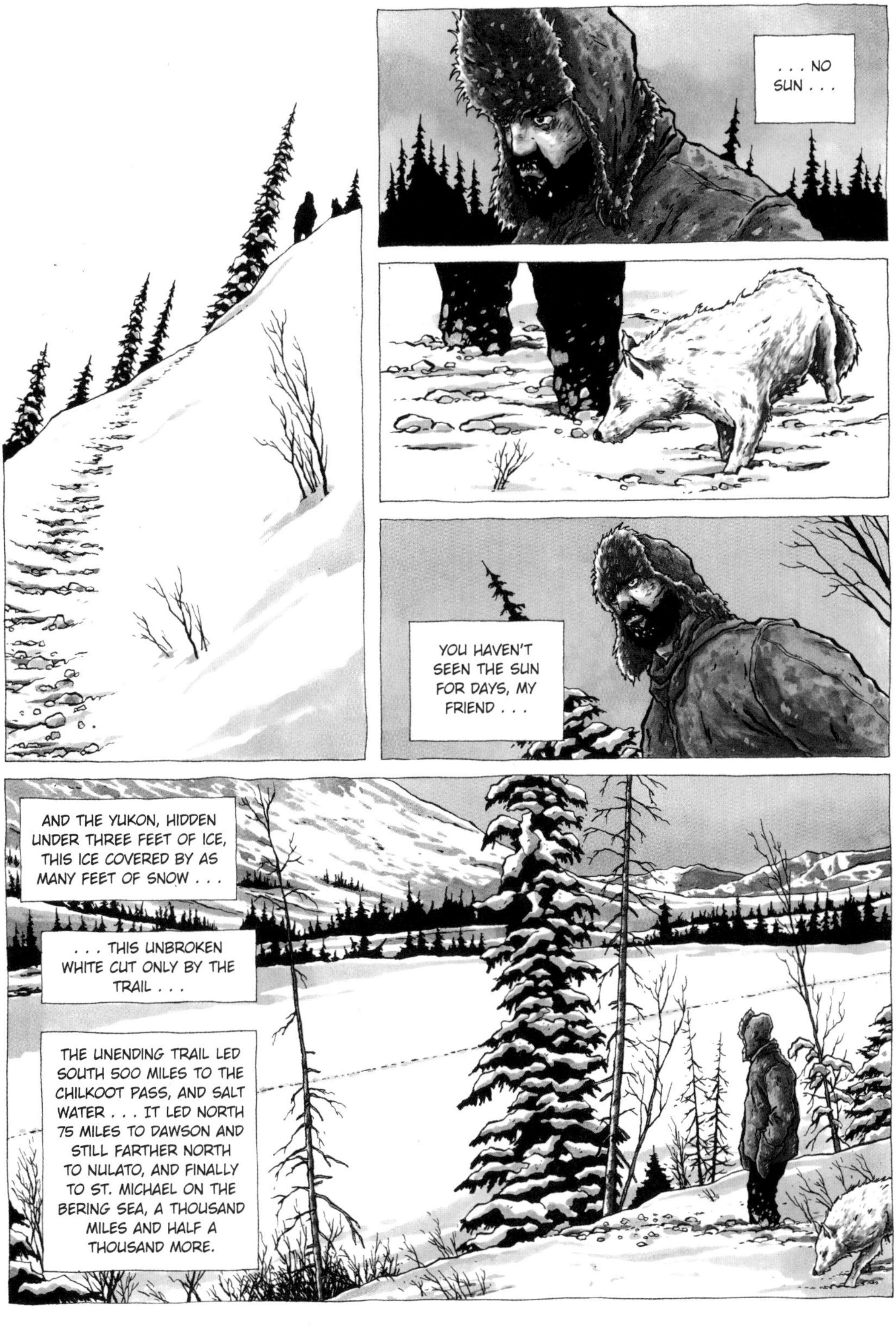
. . . NO SUN . . .
YOU HAVEN'T SEEN THE SUN FOR DAYS, MY FRIEND . . .
AND THE YUKON, HIDDEN UNDER THREE FEET OF ICE, THIS ICE COVERED BY AS MANY FEET OF SNOW . . .
. . . THIS UNBROKEN WHITE CUT ONLY BY THE TRAIL . . .
THE UNENDING TRAIL LED SOUTH 500 MILES TO THE CHILKOOT PASS, AND SALT WATER . . . IT LED NORTH 75 MILES TO DAWSON AND STILL FARTHER NORTH TO NULATO, AND FINALLY TO ST. MICHAEL ON THE BERING SEA, A THOUSAND MILES AND HALF A THOUSAND MORE.

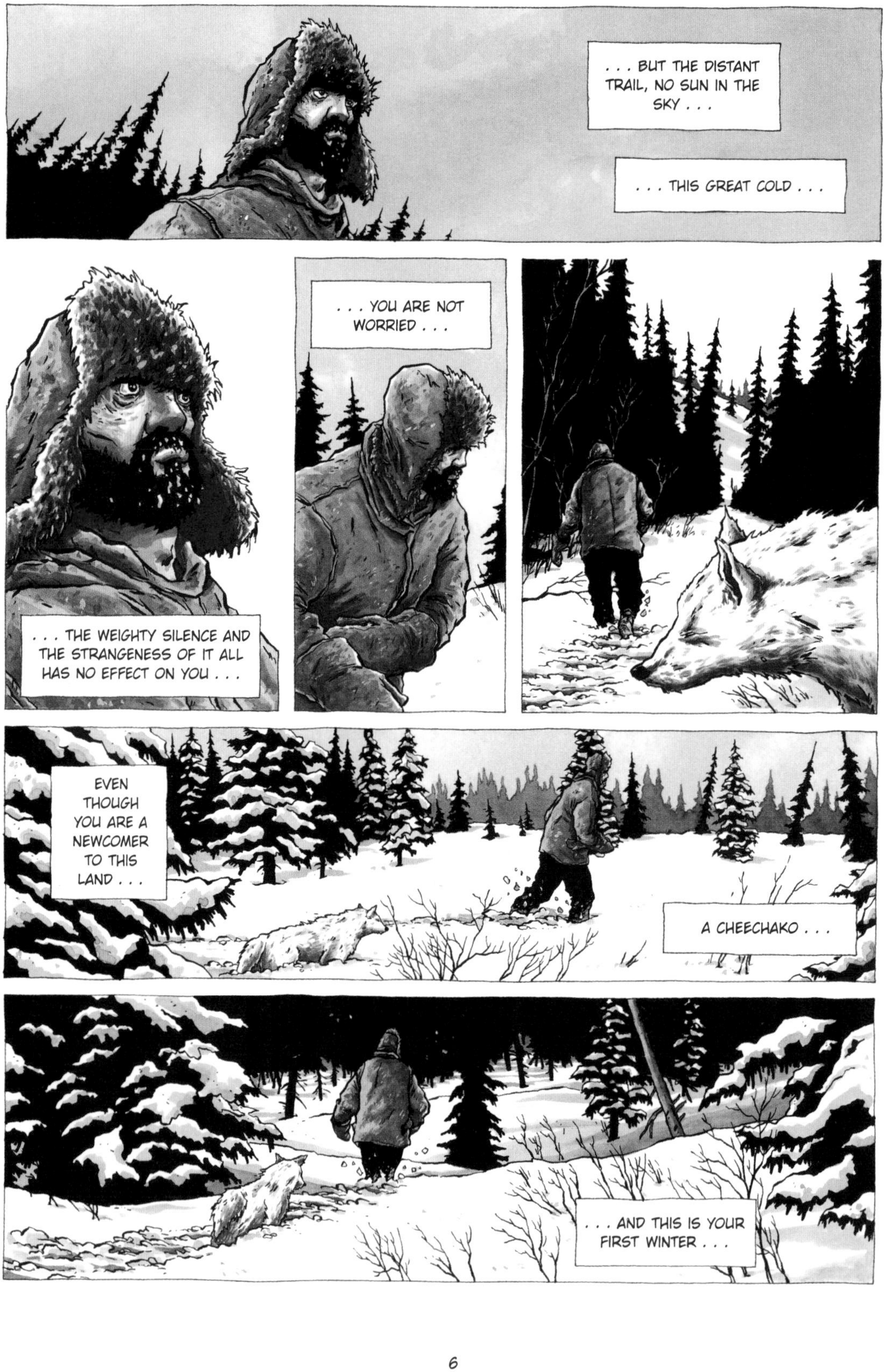
. . . BUT THE DISTANT TRAIL, NO SUN IN THE SKY . . .
. . . THIS GREAT COLD . . .
. . . THE WEIGHTY SILENCE AND THE STRANGENESS OF IT ALL HAS NO EFFECT ON YOU . . .
. . . YOU ARE NOT WORRIED . . .
EVEN THOUGH YOU ARE A NEWCOMER TO THIS LAND . . .
A CHEECHAKO . . .
. . . AND THIS IS YOUR FIRST WINTER . . .

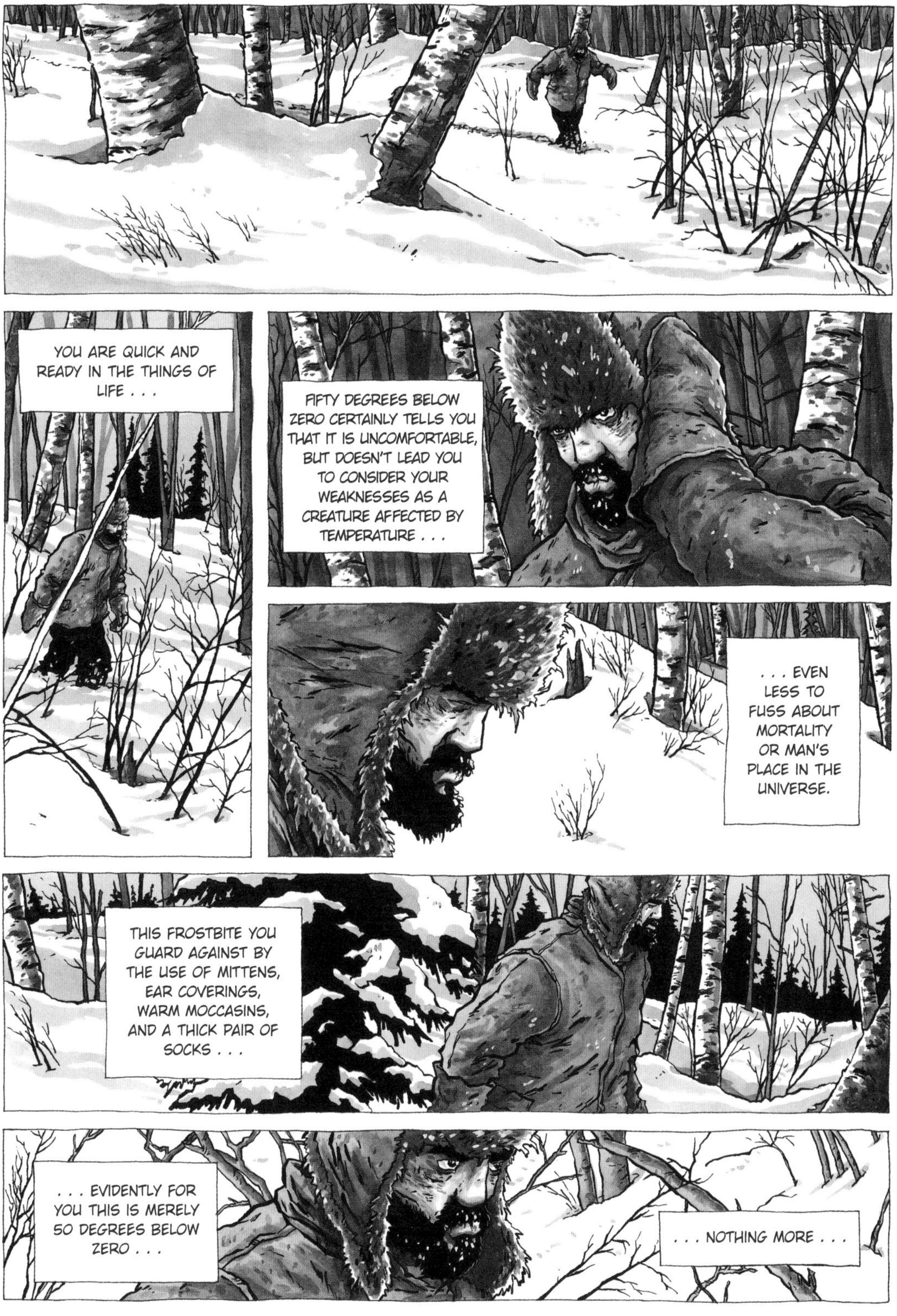
YOU ARE QUICK AND READY IN THE THINGS OF LIFE . . .
FIFTY DEGREES BELOW ZERO CERTAINLY TELLS YOU THAT IT IS UNCOMFORTABLE, BUT DOESN'T LEAD YOU TO CONSIDER YOUR WEAKNESSES AS A CREATURE AFFECTED BY TEMPERATURE . . .
. . . EVEN LESS TO FUSS ABOUT MORTALITY OR MAN'S PLACE IN THE UNIVERSE.
THIS FROSTBITE YOU GUARD AGAINST BY THE USE OF MITTENS, EAR COVERINGS, WARM MOCCASINS, AND A THICK PAIR OF SOCKS . . .
. . . EVIDENTLY FOR YOU THIS IS MERELY 50 DEGREES BELOW ZERO . . .
. . . NOTHING MORE . . .

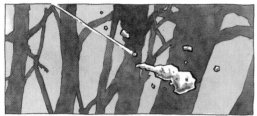
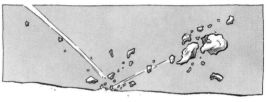

YES, MY FRIEND . . .

. . . THIS IS WHAT HAPPENS WHEN IT IS COLDER THAN 50 DEGREES BELOW ZERO . . .

YOUR SPIT SHOULD FREEZE ONLY WHEN IT HITS THE GROUND . . .

. . . BUT LOOK, IT SOLIDIFIES AT SIMPLE AIR CONTACT . . .

. . . IN MIDFLIGHT . . .

. . . BUT YOU LAUGH AT THE TEMPERATURE . . .

. . . FOR YOU, IT DOES NOT MATTER . . .

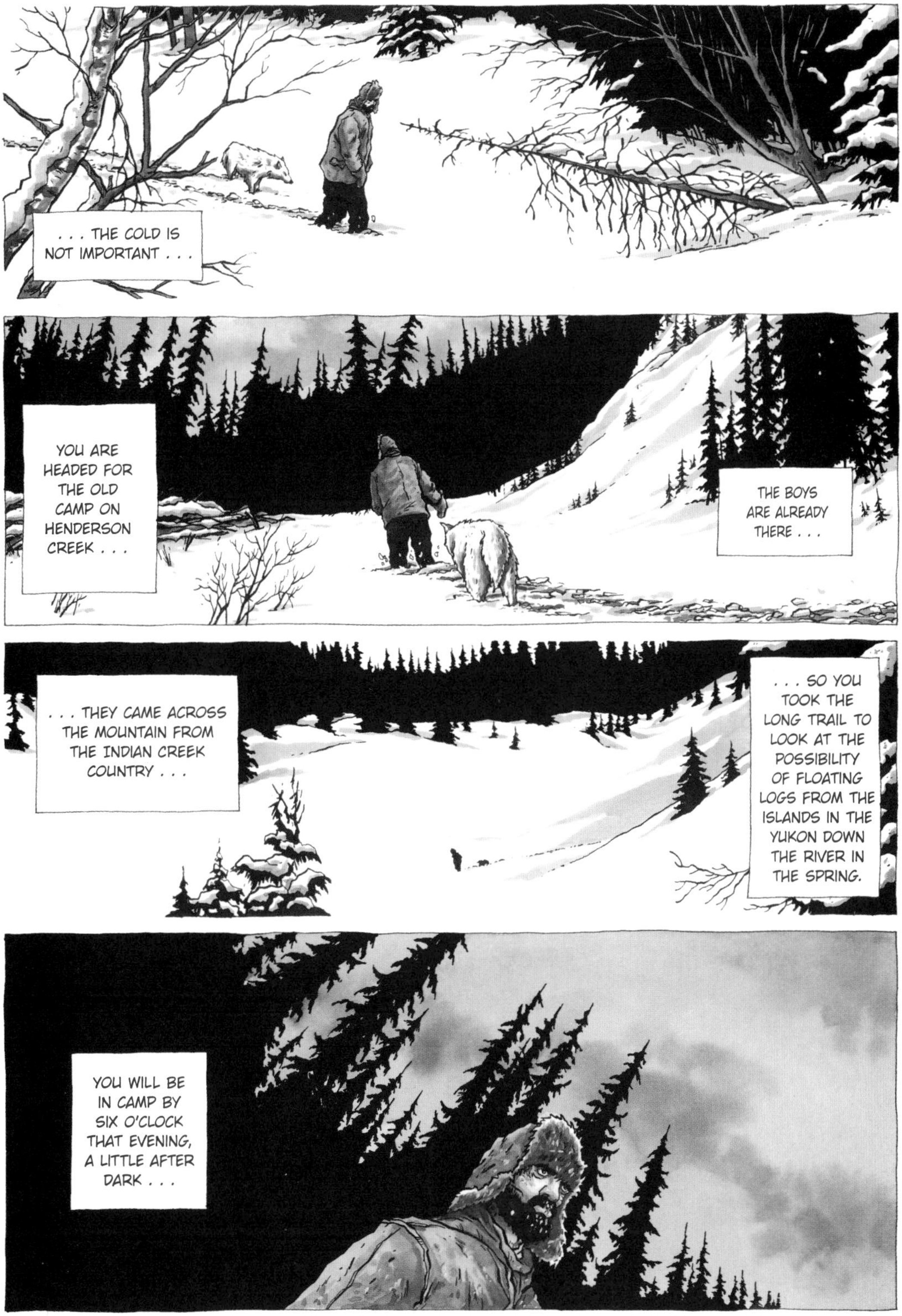
. . . THE COLD IS NOT IMPORTANT . . .
YOU ARE HEADED FOR THE OLD CAMP ON HENDERSON CREEK . . .
THE BOYS ARE ALREADY THERE . . .
. . . THEY CAME ACROSS THE MOUNTAIN FROM THE INDIAN CREEK COUNTRY . . .
. . . SO YOU TOOK THE LONG TRAIL TO LOOK AT THE POSSIBILITY OF FLOATING LOGS FROM THE ISLANDS IN THE YUKON DOWN THE RIVER IN THE SPRING.
YOU WILL BE IN CAMP BY SIX O'CLOCK THAT EVENING, A LITTLE AFTER DARK . . .

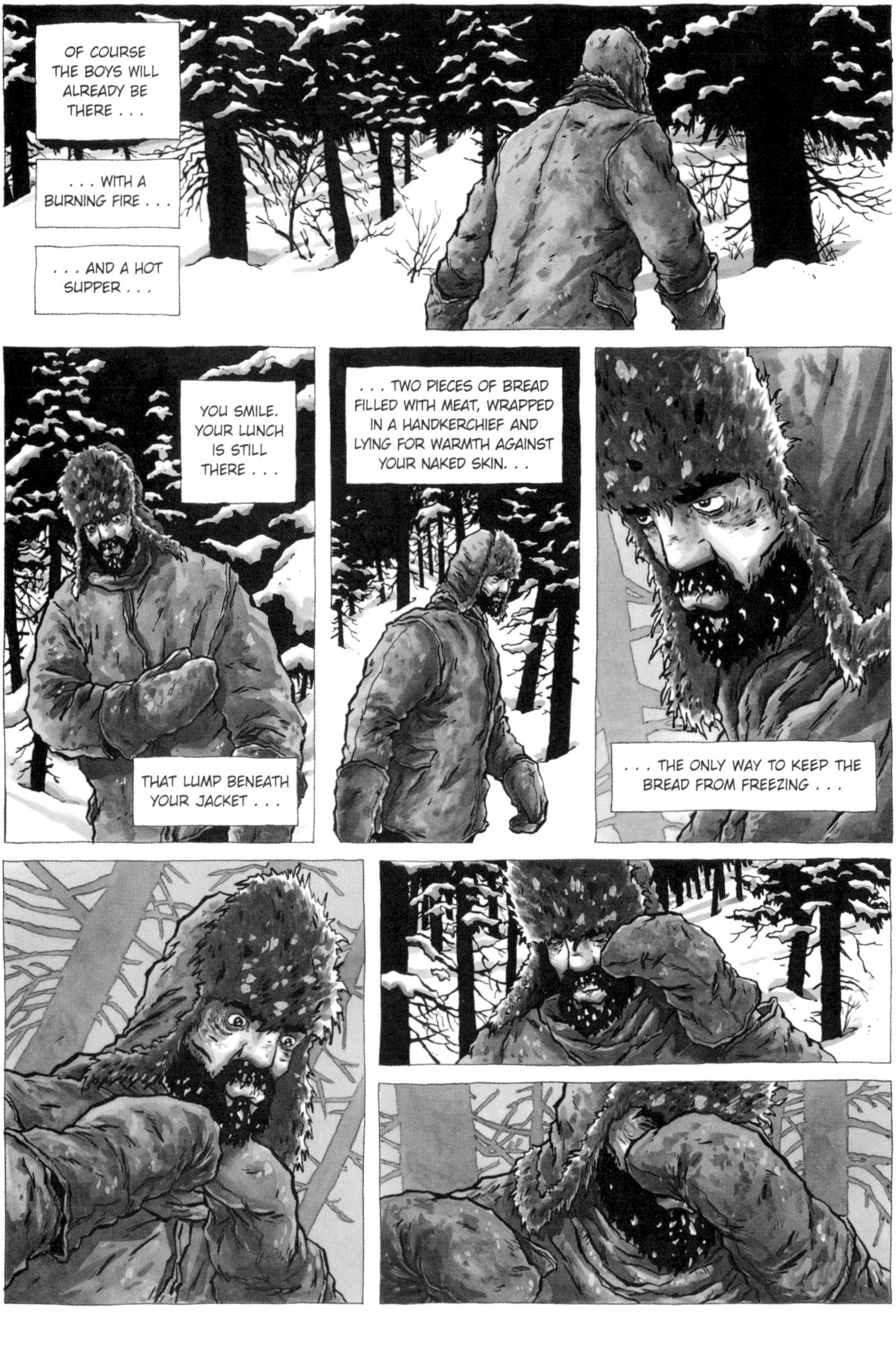
OF COURSE THE BOYS WILL ALREADY BE THERE . . .
. . . WITH A BURNING FIRE . . .
. . . AND A HOT SUPPER . . .
YOU SMILE. YOUR LUNCH IS STILL THERE . . .
THAT LUMP BENEATH YOUR JACKET . . .
. . . TWO PIECES OF BREAD FILLED WITH MEAT, WRAPPED IN A HANDKERCHIEF AND LYING FOR WARMTH AGAINST YOUR NAKED SKIN. . .
. . . THE ONLY WAY TO KEEP THE BREAD FROM FREEZING . . .

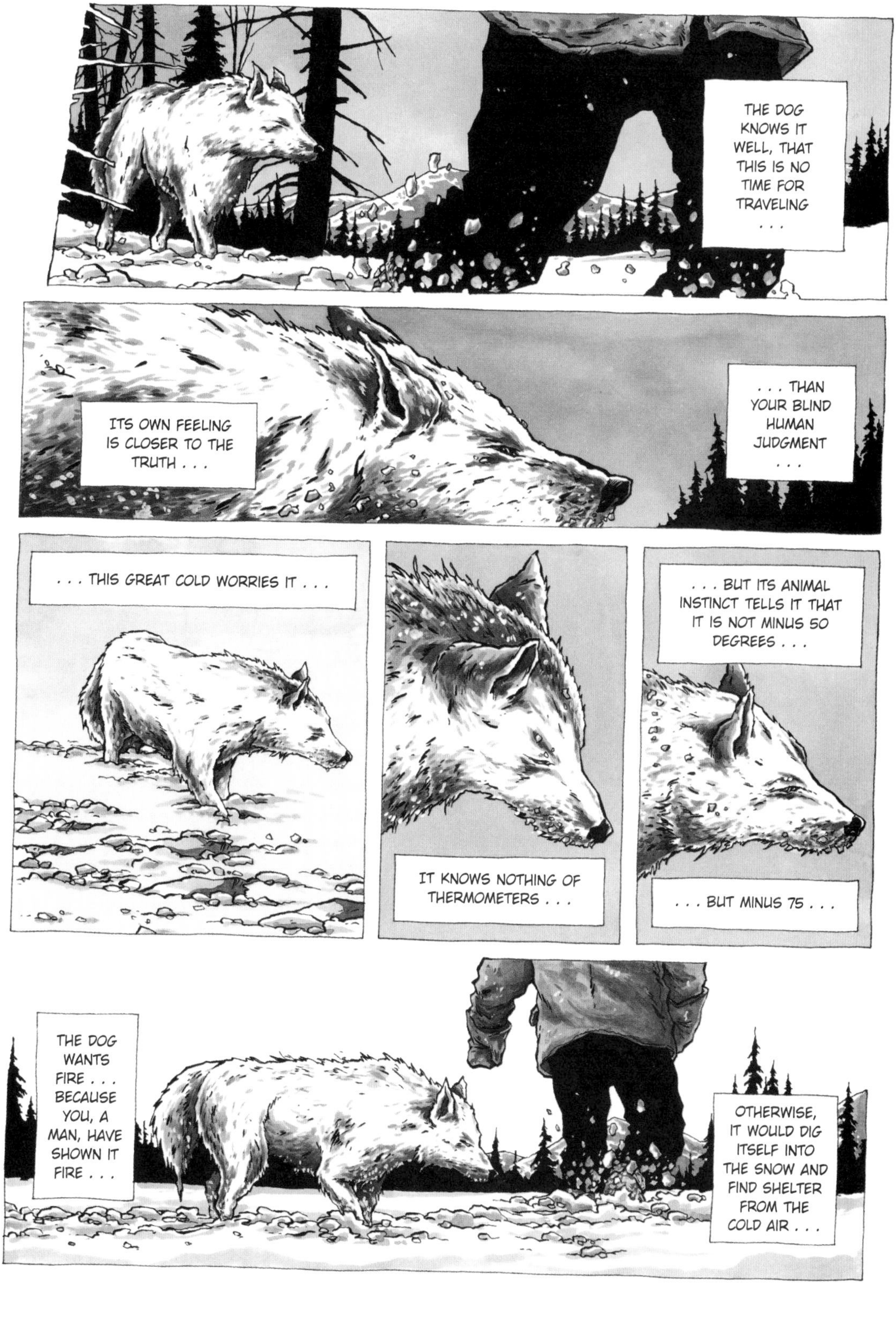
THE DOG KNOWS IT WELL, THAT THIS IS NO TIME FOR TRAVELING . . .
ITS OWN FEELING IS CLOSER TO THE TRUTH . . .
. . . THAN YOUR BLIND HUMAN JUDGMENT . . .
. . . THIS GREAT COLD WORRIES IT . . .
IT KNOWS NOTHING OF THERMOMETERS . . .
. . . BUT ITS ANIMAL INSTINCT TELLS IT THAT IT IS NOT MINUS 50 DEGREES . . .
. . . BUT MINUS 75 . . .
THE DOG WANTS FIRE . . . BECAUSE YOU, A MAN, HAVE SHOWN IT FIRE . . .
OTHERWISE, IT WOULD DIG ITSELF INTO THE SNOW AND FIND SHELTER FROM THE COLD AIR . . .

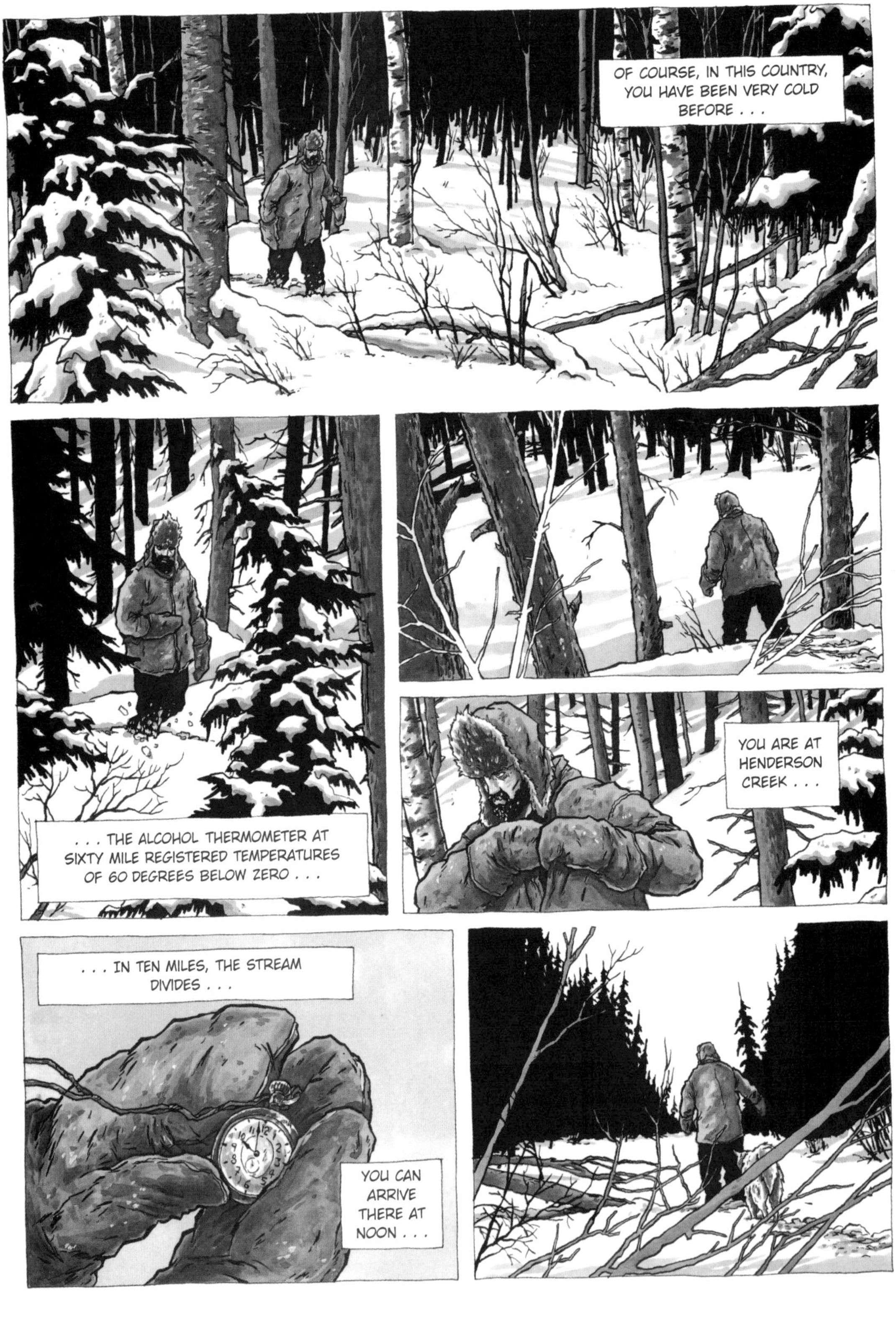
OF COURSE, IN THIS COUNTRY, YOU HAVE BEEN VERY COLD BEFORE . . .
. . . THE ALCOHOL THERMOMETER AT SIXTY MILE REGISTERED TEMPERATURES OF 60 DEGREES BELOW ZERO . . .
YOU ARE AT HENDERSON CREEK . . .
. . . IN TEN MILES, THE STREAM DIVIDES . . .
YOU CAN ARRIVE THERE AT NOON . . .

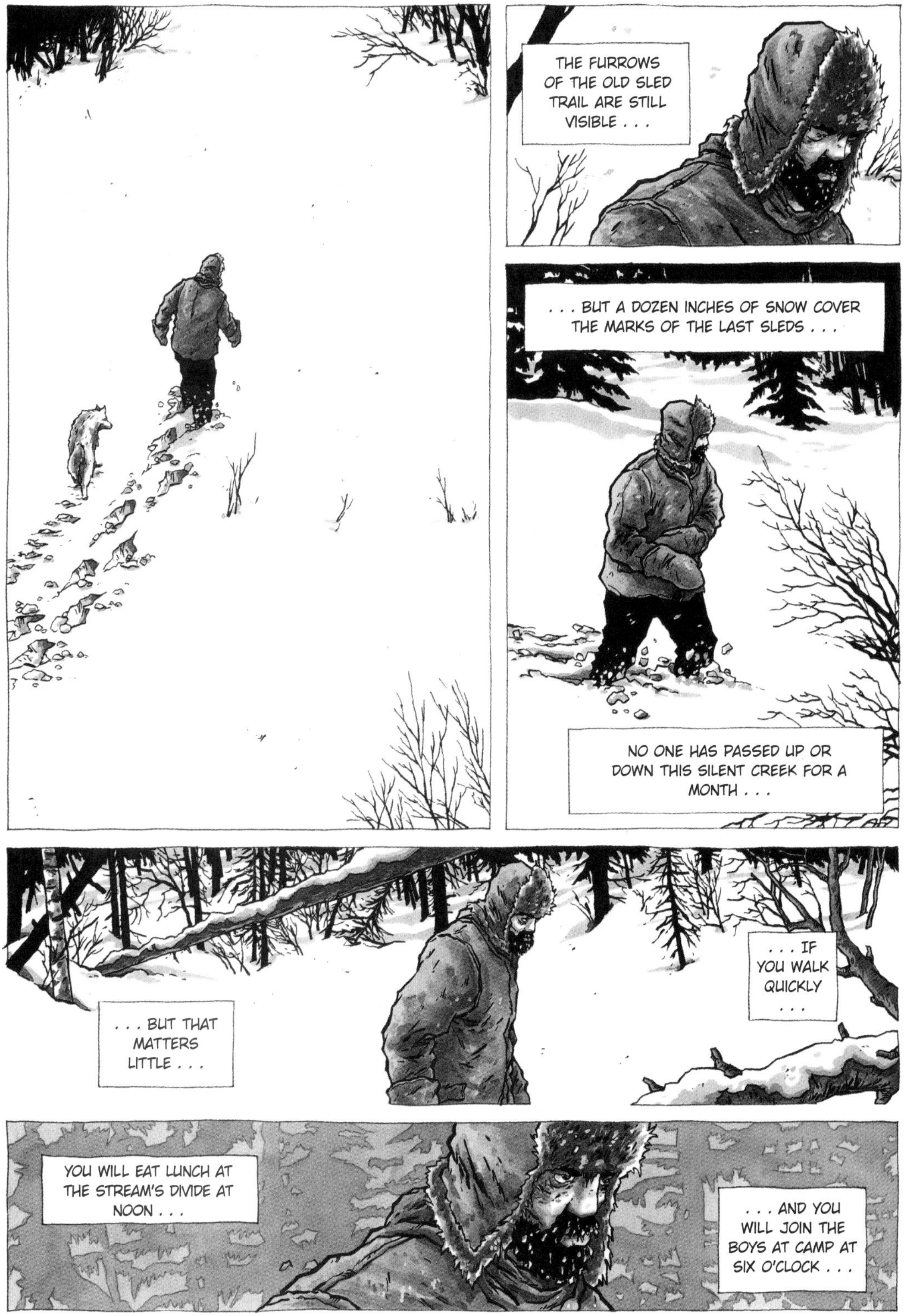
THE FURROWS OF THE OLD SLED TRAIL ARE STILL VISIBLE . . .
. . . BUT A DOZEN INCHES OF SNOW COVER THE MARKS OF THE LAST SLEDS . . .
NO ONE HAS PASSED UP OR DOWN THIS SILENT CREEK FOR A MONTH . . .
. . . BUT THAT MATTERS LITTLE . . .
. . . IF YOU WALK QUICKLY . . .
YOU WILL EAT LUNCH AT THE STREAM'S DIVIDE AT NOON . . .
. . . AND YOU WILL JOIN THE BOYS AT CAMP AT SIX O'CLOCK . . .

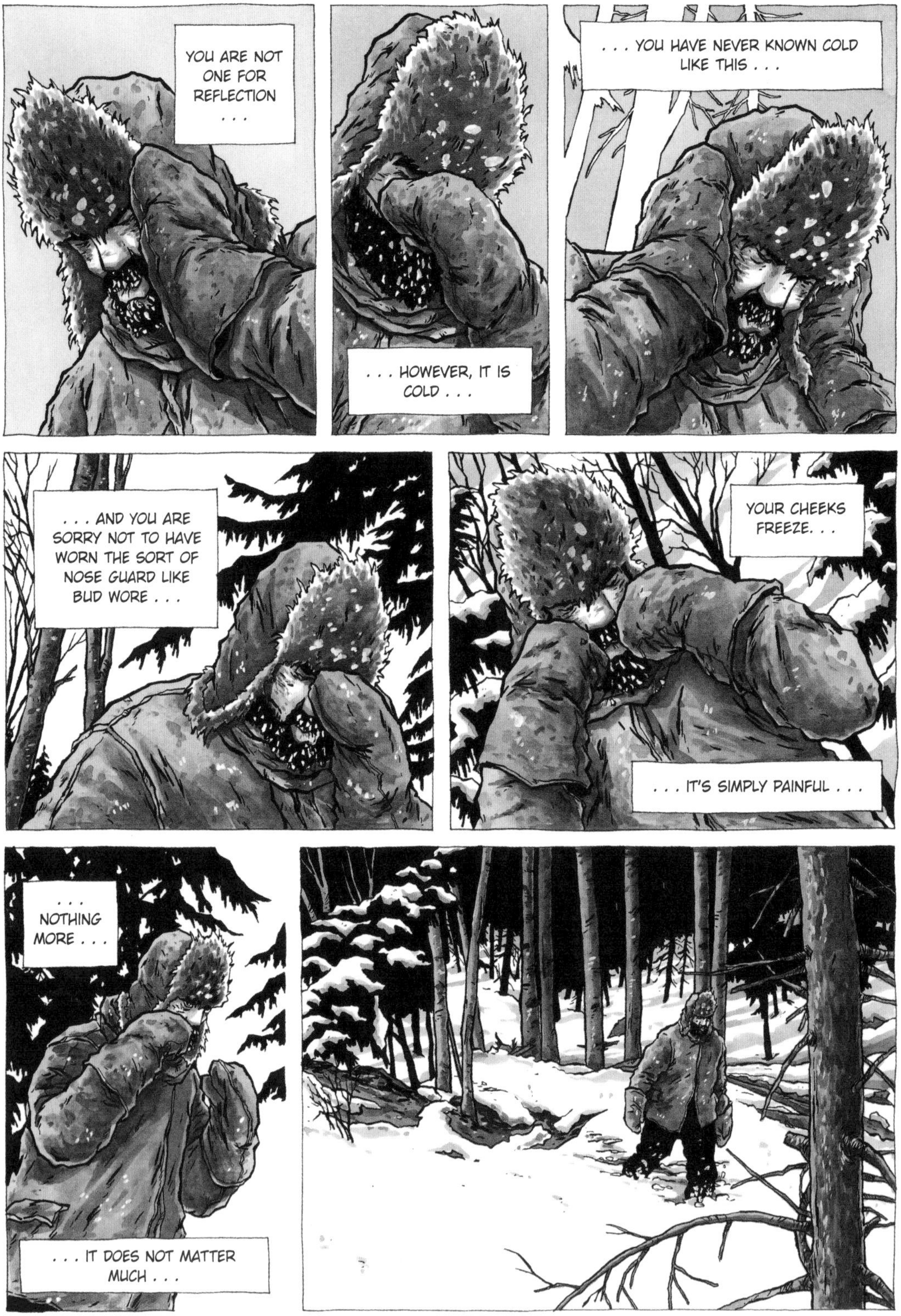
YOU ARE NOT ONE FOR REFLECTION . . .
. . . HOWEVER, IT IS COLD . . .
. . . YOU HAVE NEVER KNOWN COLD LIKE THIS . . .
. . . AND YOU ARE SORRY NOT TO HAVE WORN THE SORT OF NOSE GUARD LIKE BUD WORE . . .
YOUR CHEEKS FREEZE. . .
. . . IT'S SIMPLY PAINFUL . . .
. . . NOTHING MORE . . .
. . . IT DOES NOT MATTER MUCH . . .

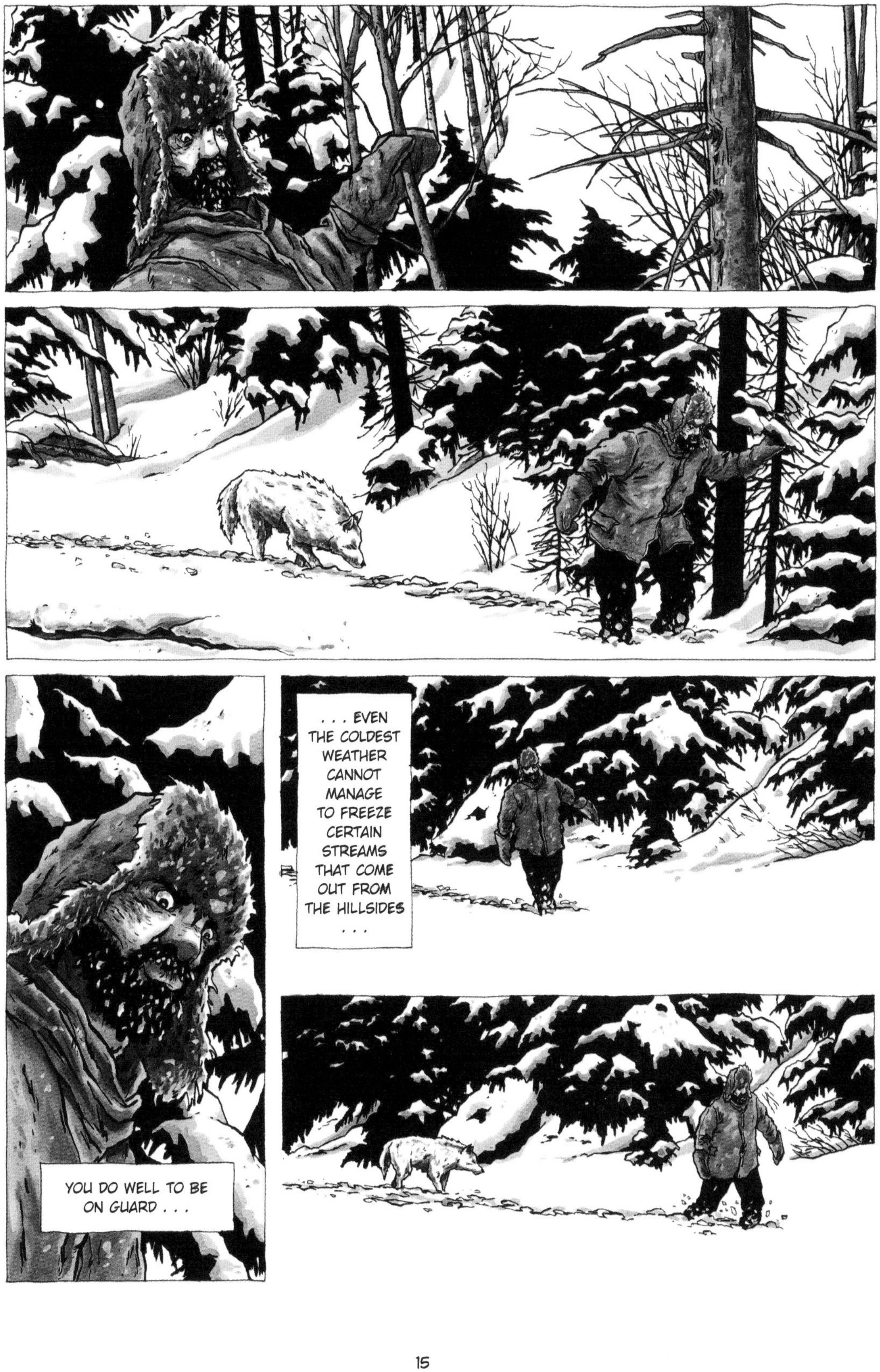
YOU DO WELL TO BE ON GUARD . . .
. . . EVEN THE COLDEST WEATHER CANNOT MANAGE TO FREEZE CERTAIN STREAMS THAT COME OUT FROM THE HILLSIDES . . .

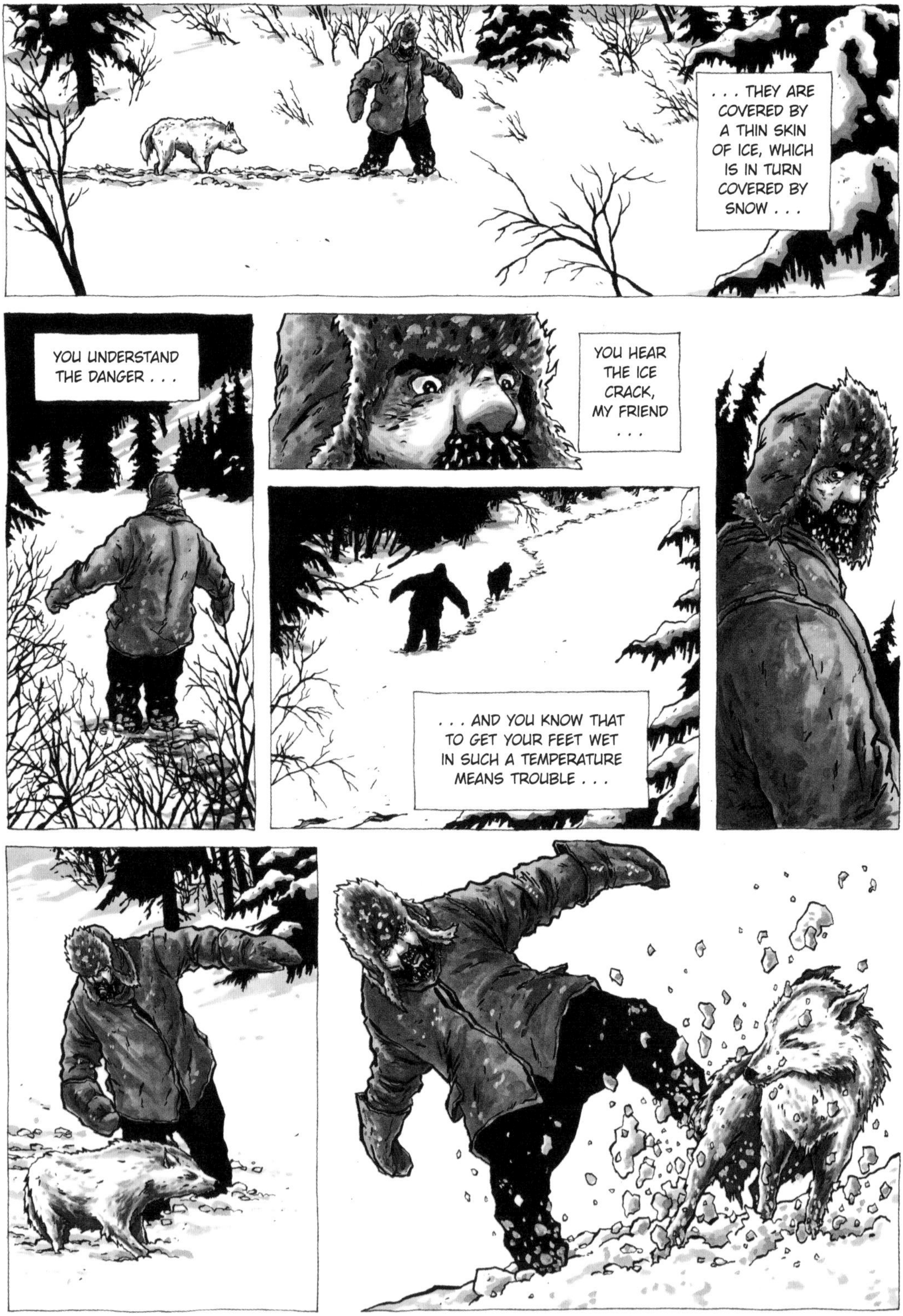
. . . THEY ARE COVERED BY A THIN SKIN OF ICE, WHICH IS IN TURN COVERED BY SNOW . . .
YOU UNDERSTAND THE DANGER . . .
YOU HEAR THE ICE CRACK, MY FRIEND . . .
. . . AND YOU KNOW THAT TO GET YOUR FEET WET IN SUCH A TEMPERATURE MEANS TROUBLE . . .

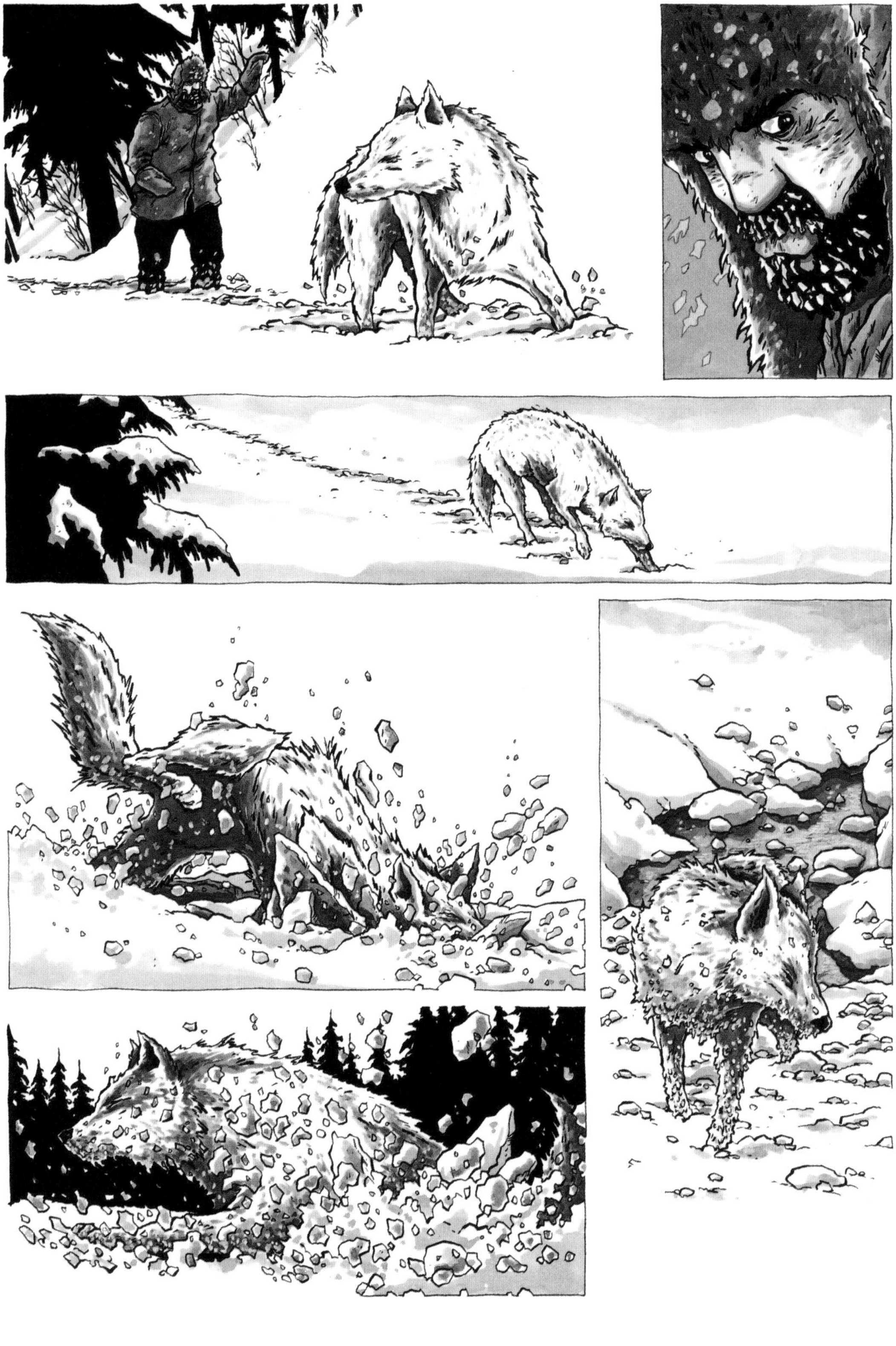

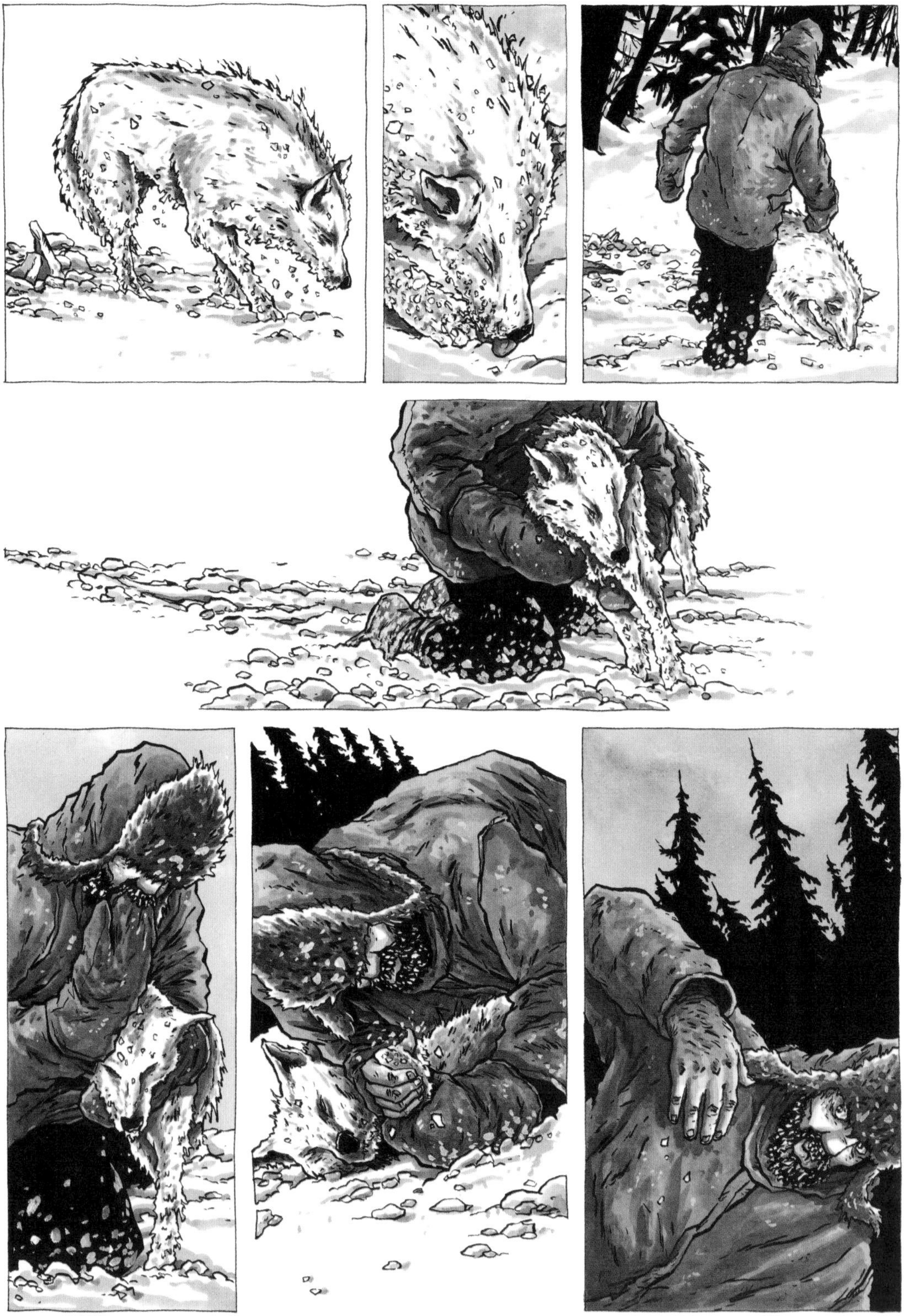

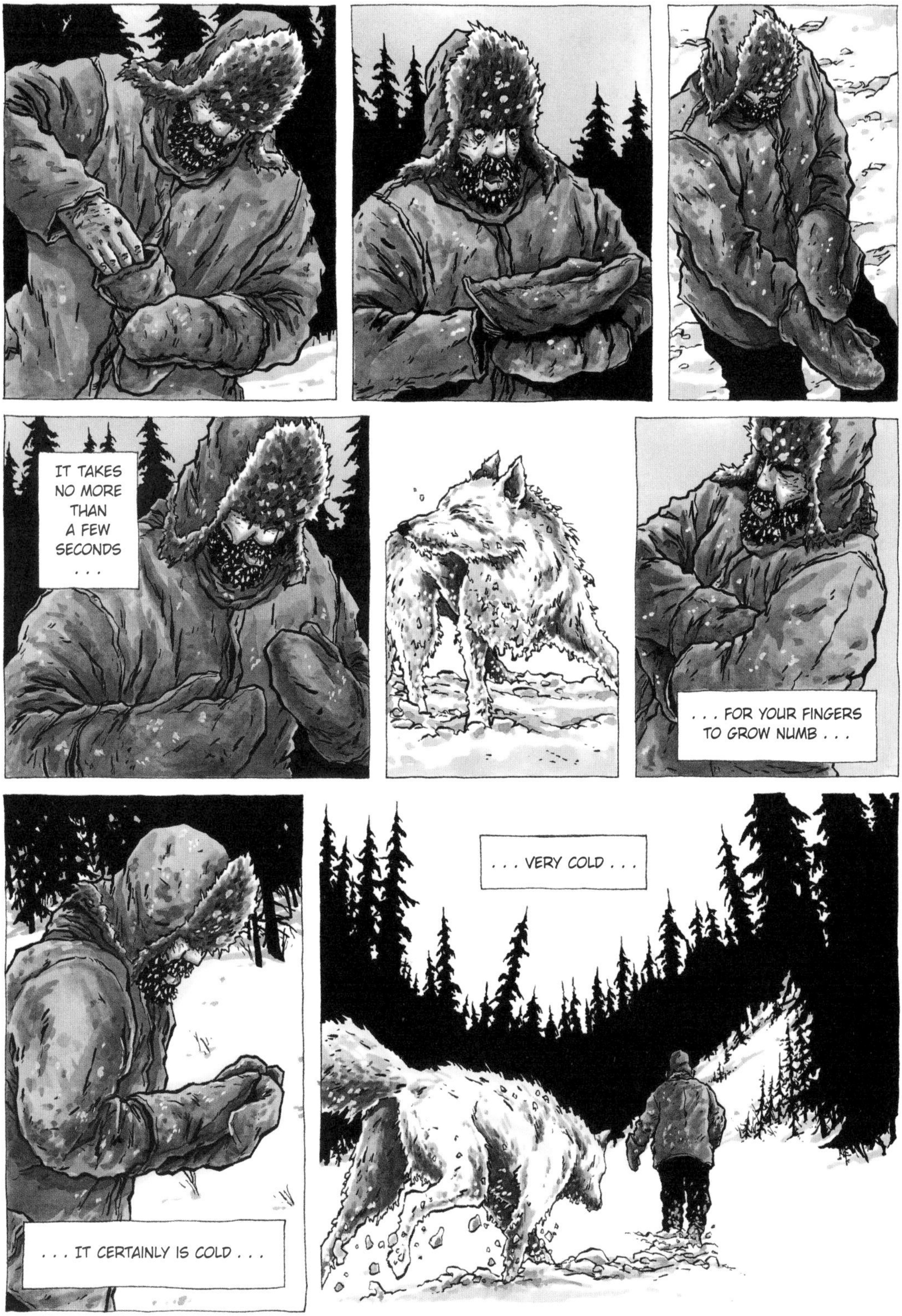
IT TAKES NO MORE THAN A FEW SECONDS . . .
. . . FOR YOUR FINGERS TO GROW NUMB . . .
. . . IT CERTAINLY IS COLD . . .
. . . VERY COLD . . .

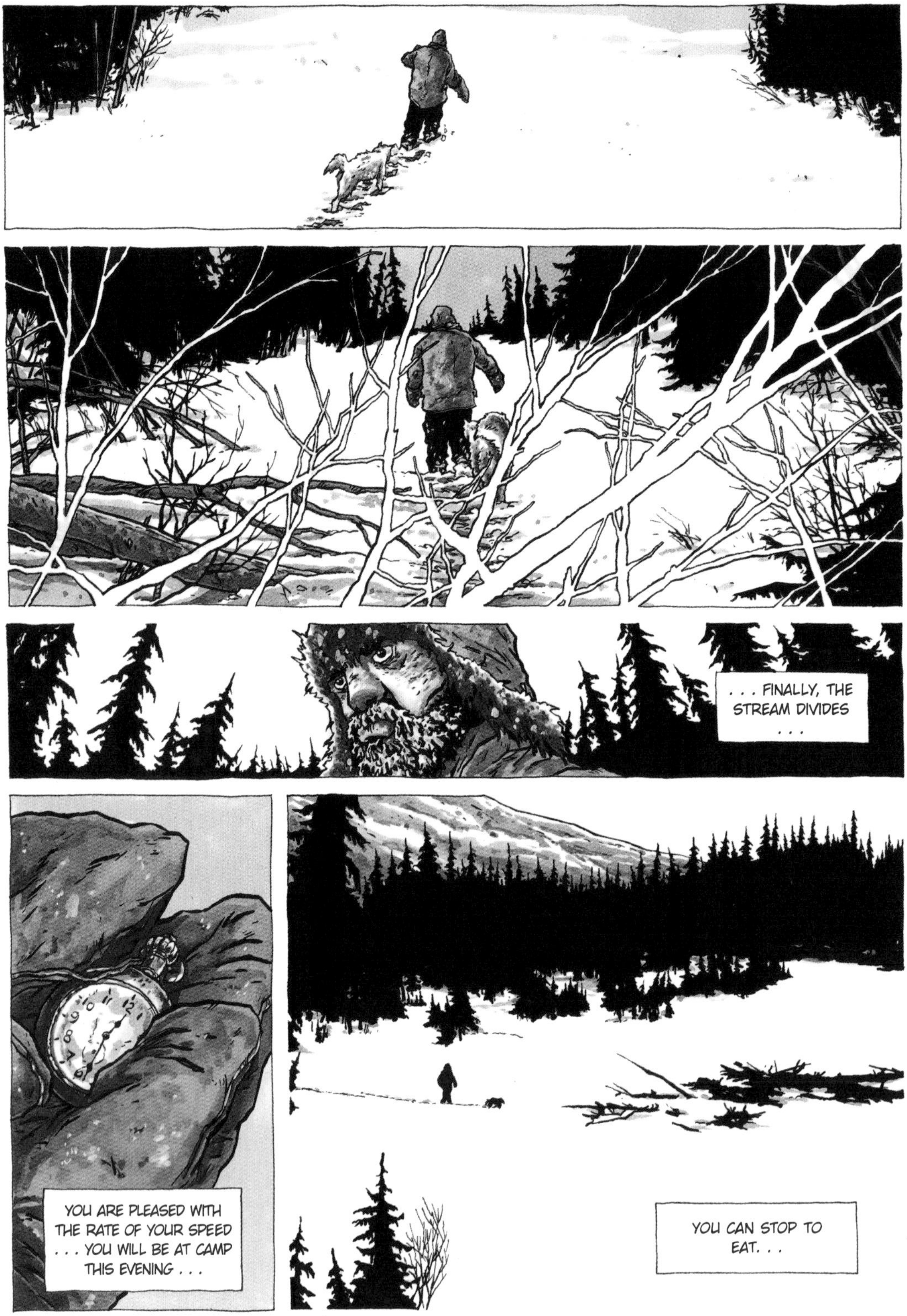
. . . FINALLY, THE STREAM DIVIDES . . .
YOU ARE PLEASED WITH THE RATE OF YOUR SPEED . . . YOU WILL BE AT CAMP THIS EVENING . . .
YOU CAN STOP TO EAT. . .

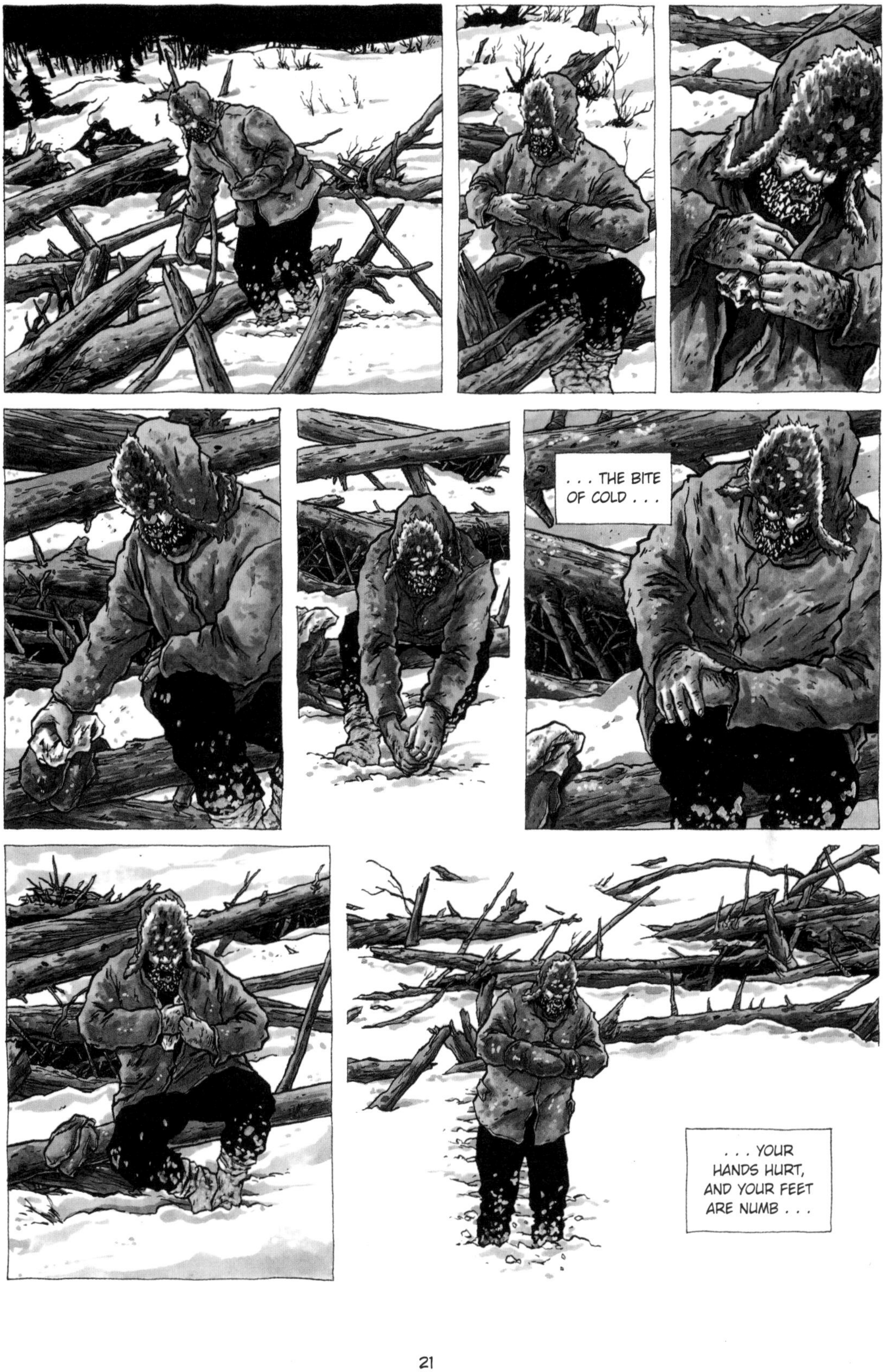
. . . THE BITE OF COLD . . .
. . . YOUR HANDS HURT, AND YOUR FEET ARE NUMB . . .

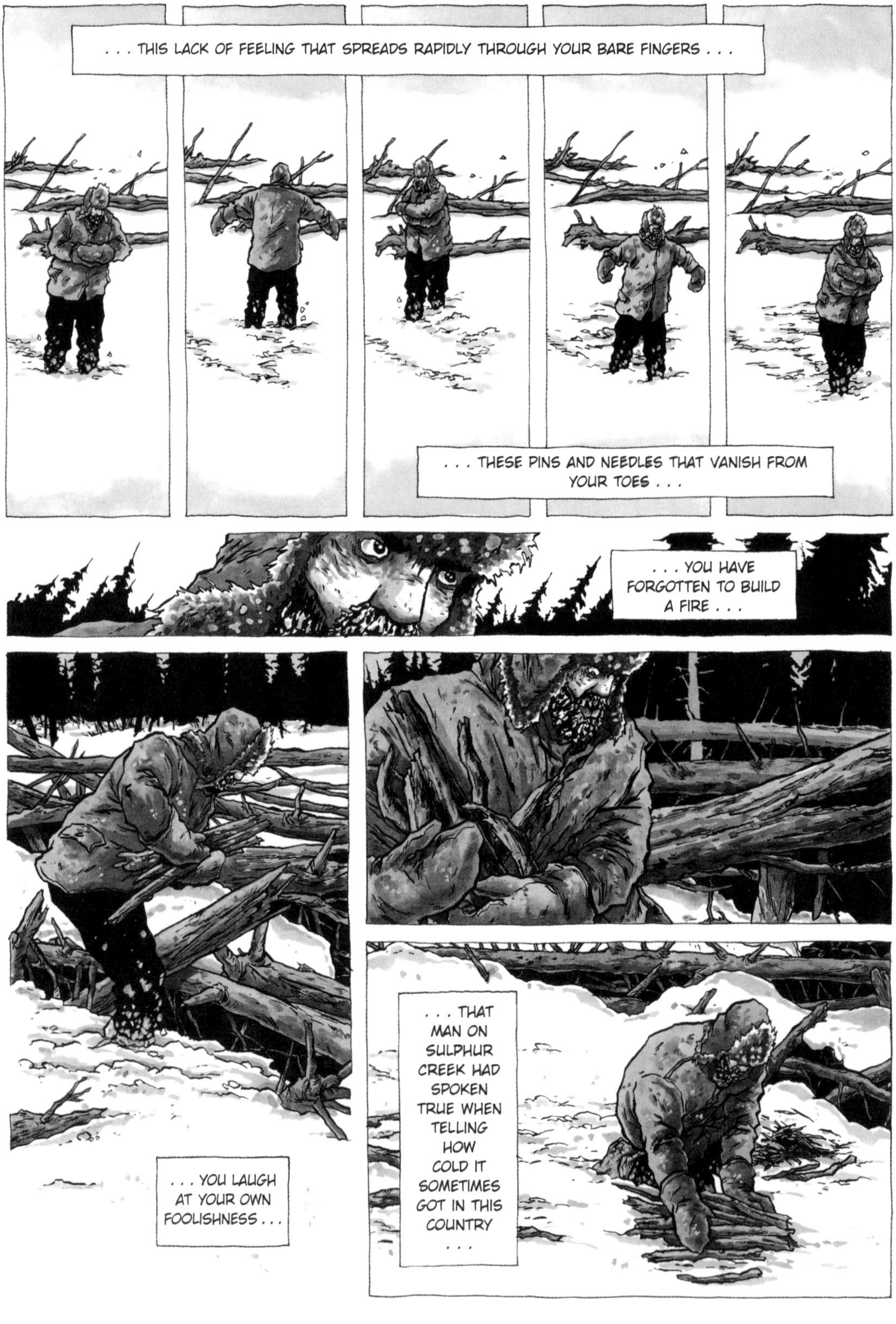

. . . THIS LACK OF FEELING THAT SPREADS RAPIDLY THROUGH YOUR BARE FINGERS . . .
. . . THESE PINS AND NEEDLES THAT VANISH FROM YOUR TOES . . .
. . . YOU HAVE FORGOTTEN TO BUILD A FIRE . . .
. . . YOU LAUGH AT YOUR OWN FOOLISHNESS . . .
. . . THAT MAN ON SULPHUR CREEK HAD SPOKEN TRUE WHEN TELLING HOW COLD IT SOMETIMES GOT IN THIS COUNTRY . . .

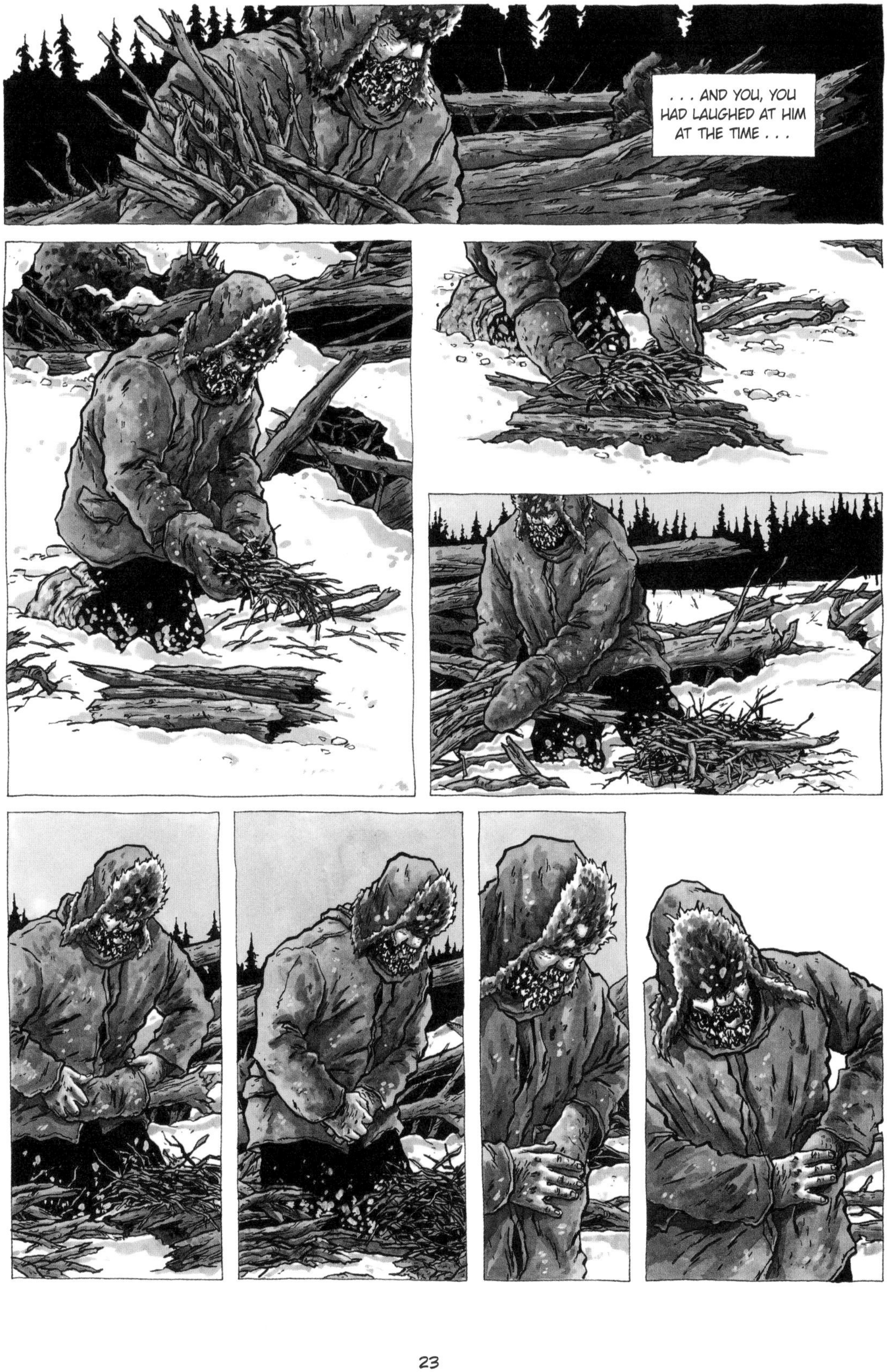
. . . AND YOU, YOU HAD LAUGHED AT HIM AT THE TIME . . .

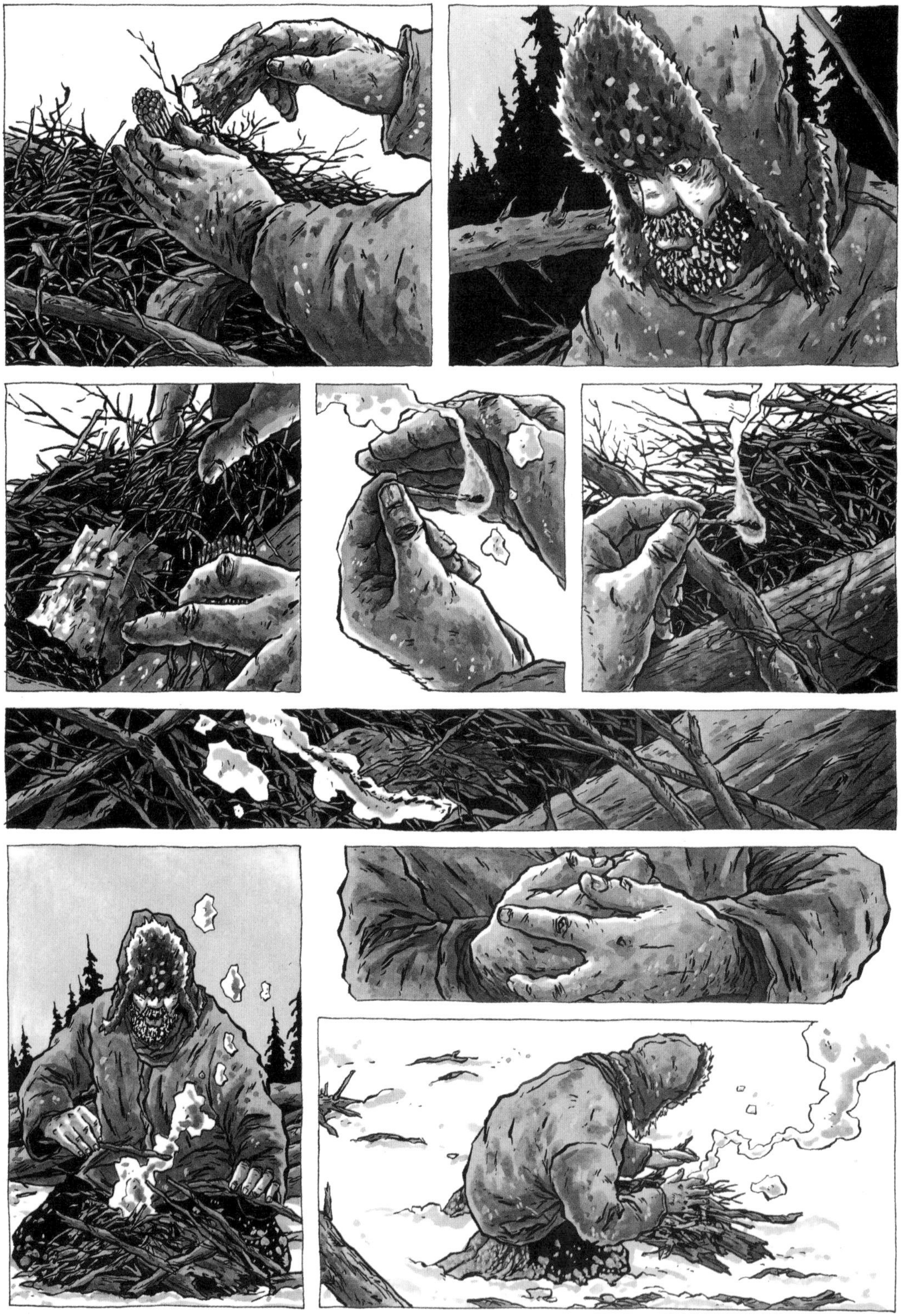

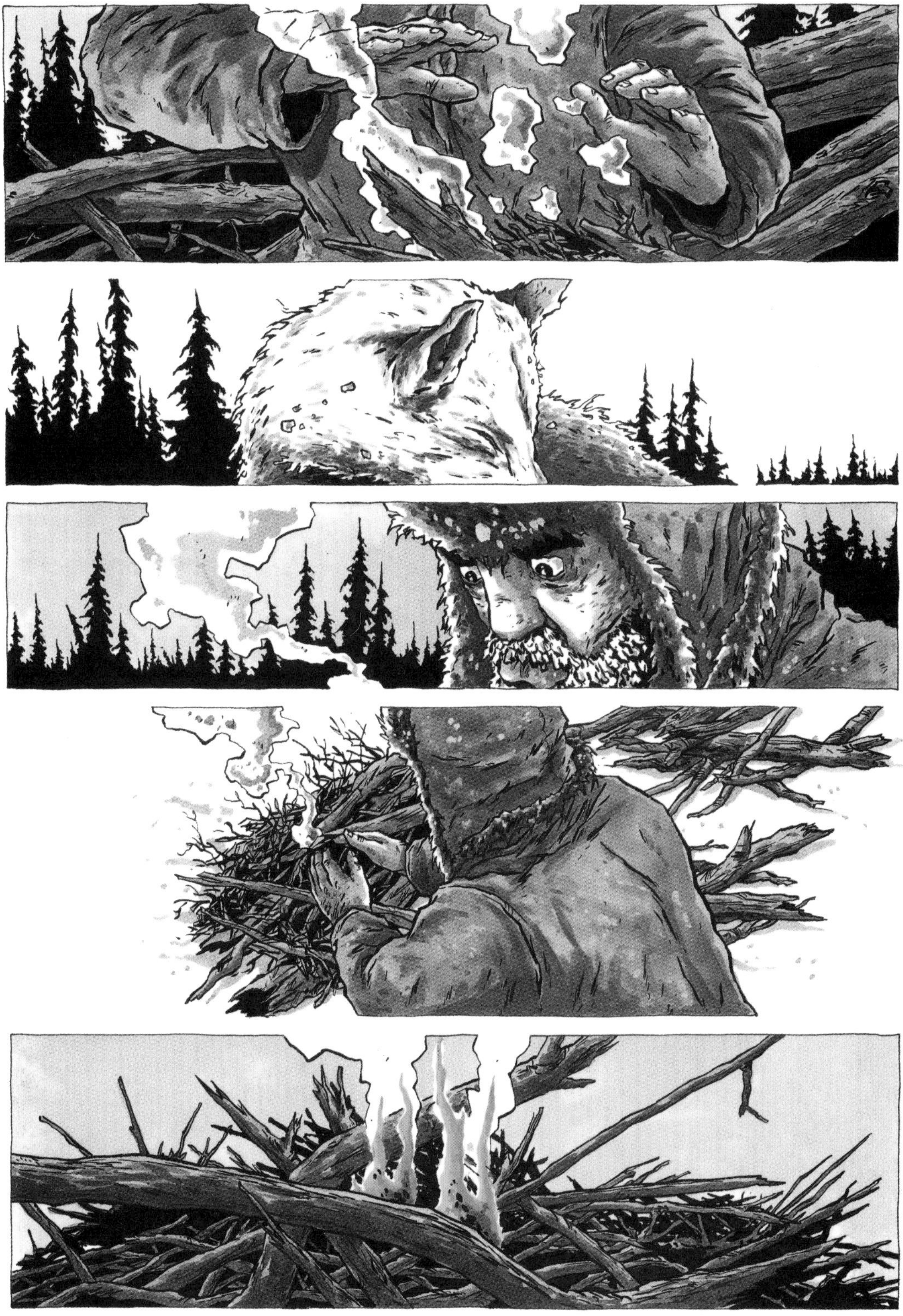

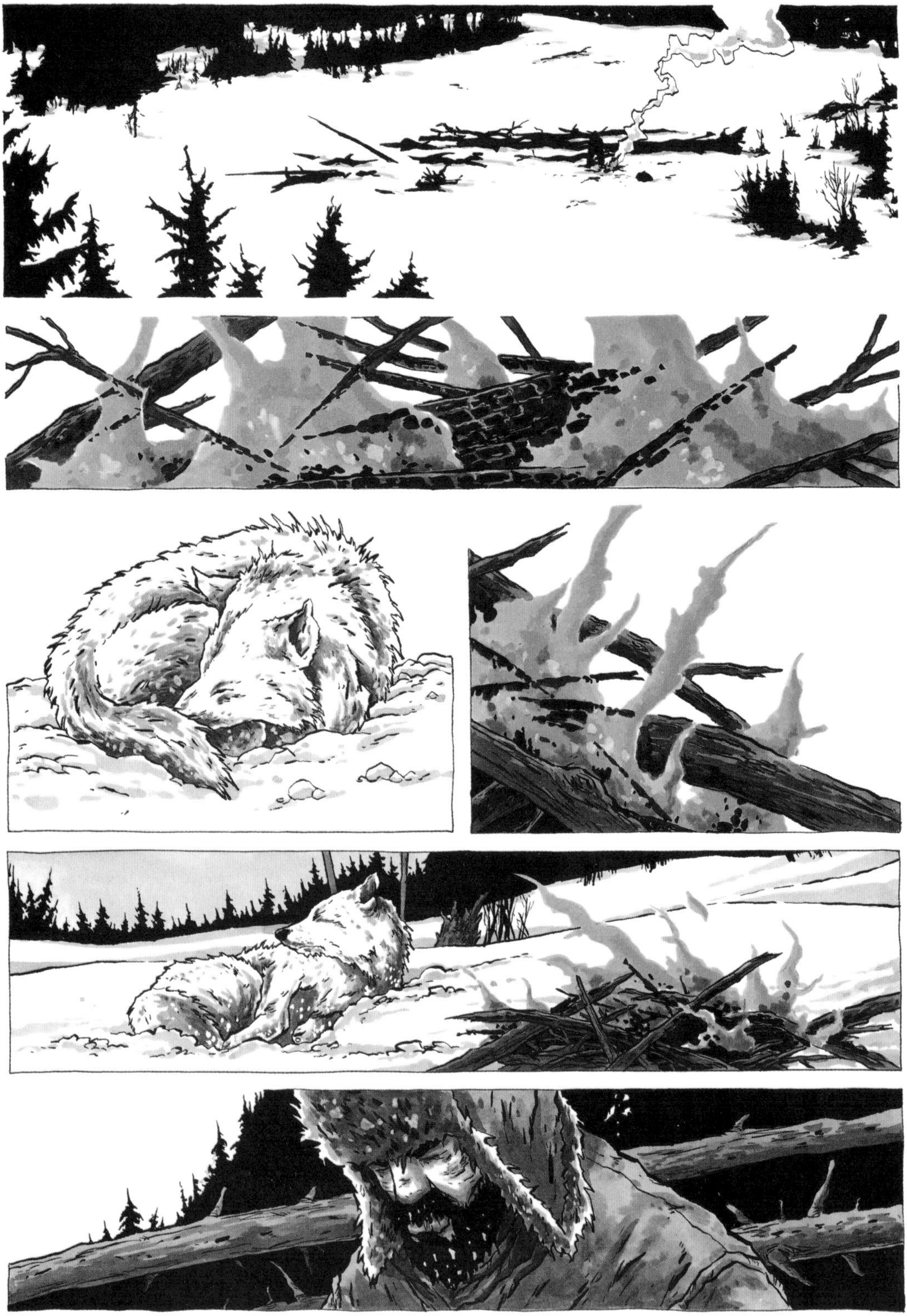

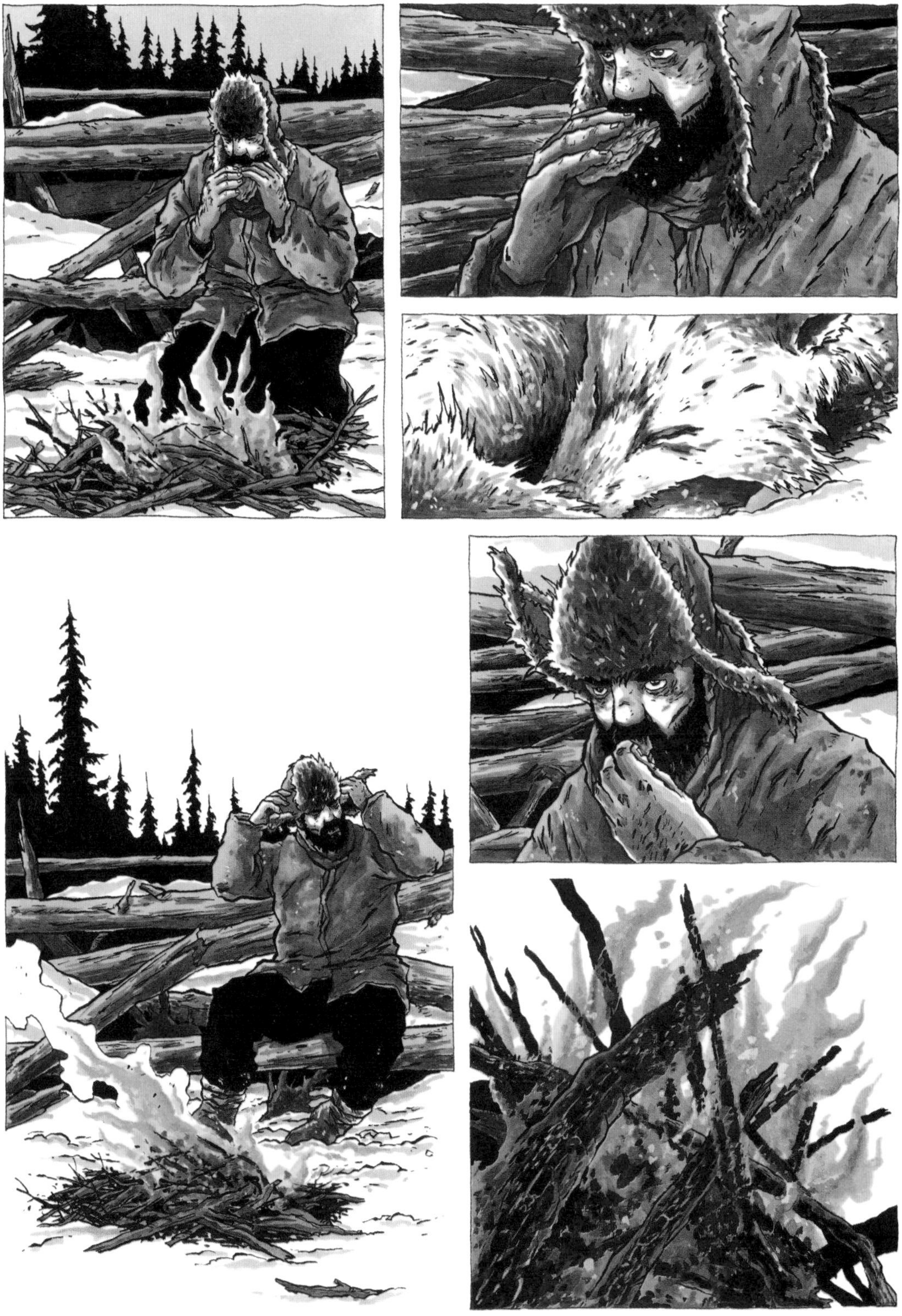

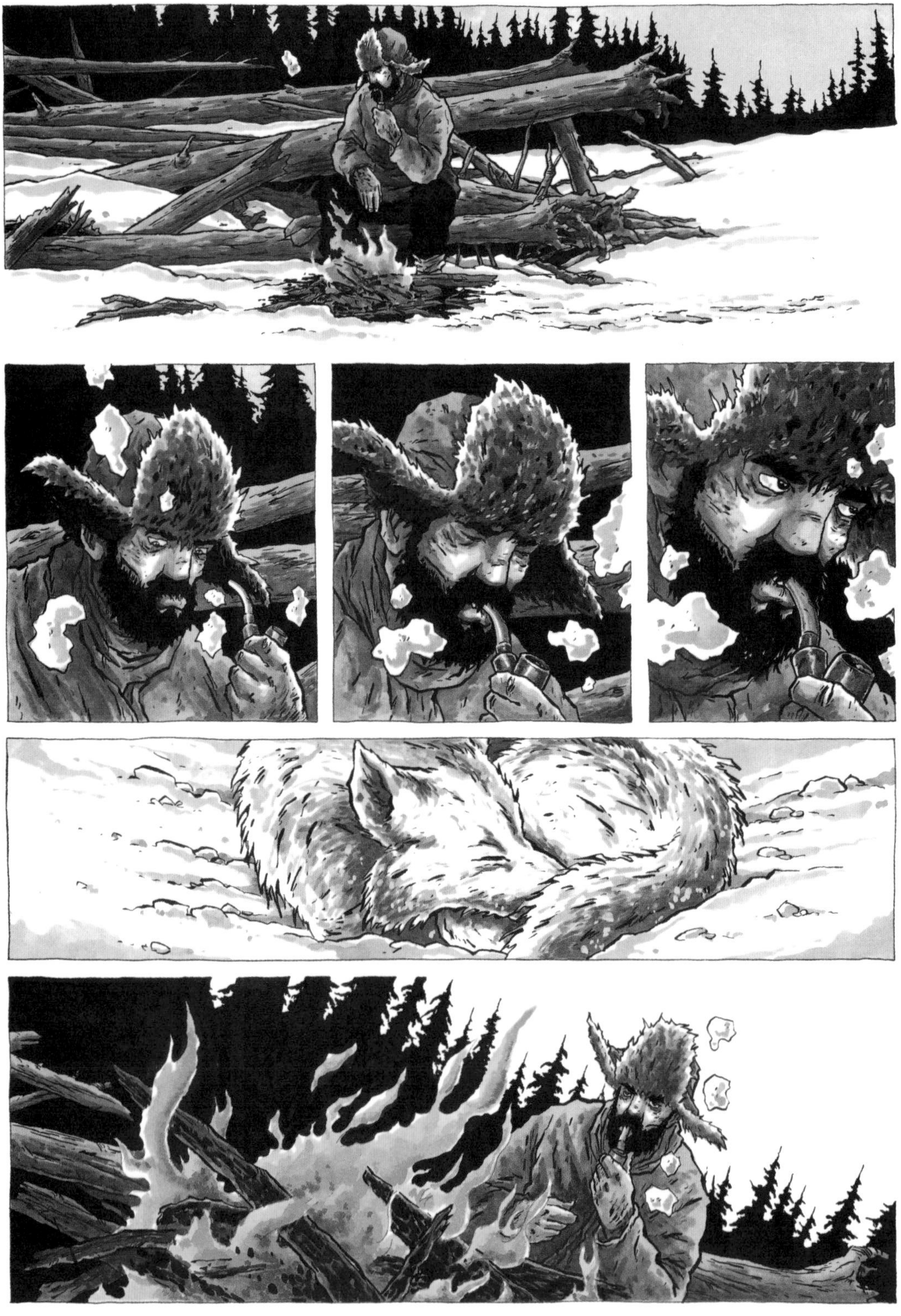

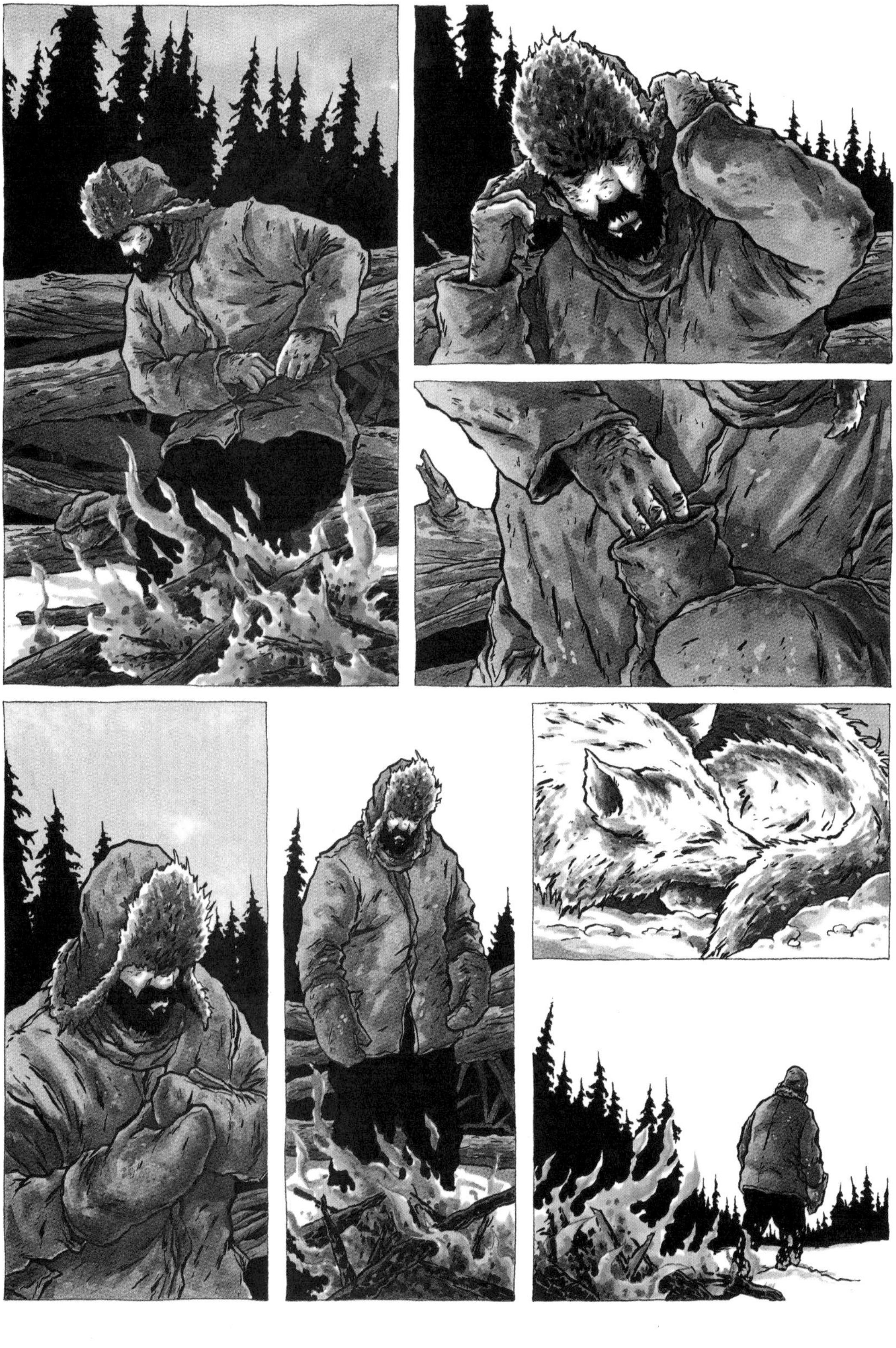

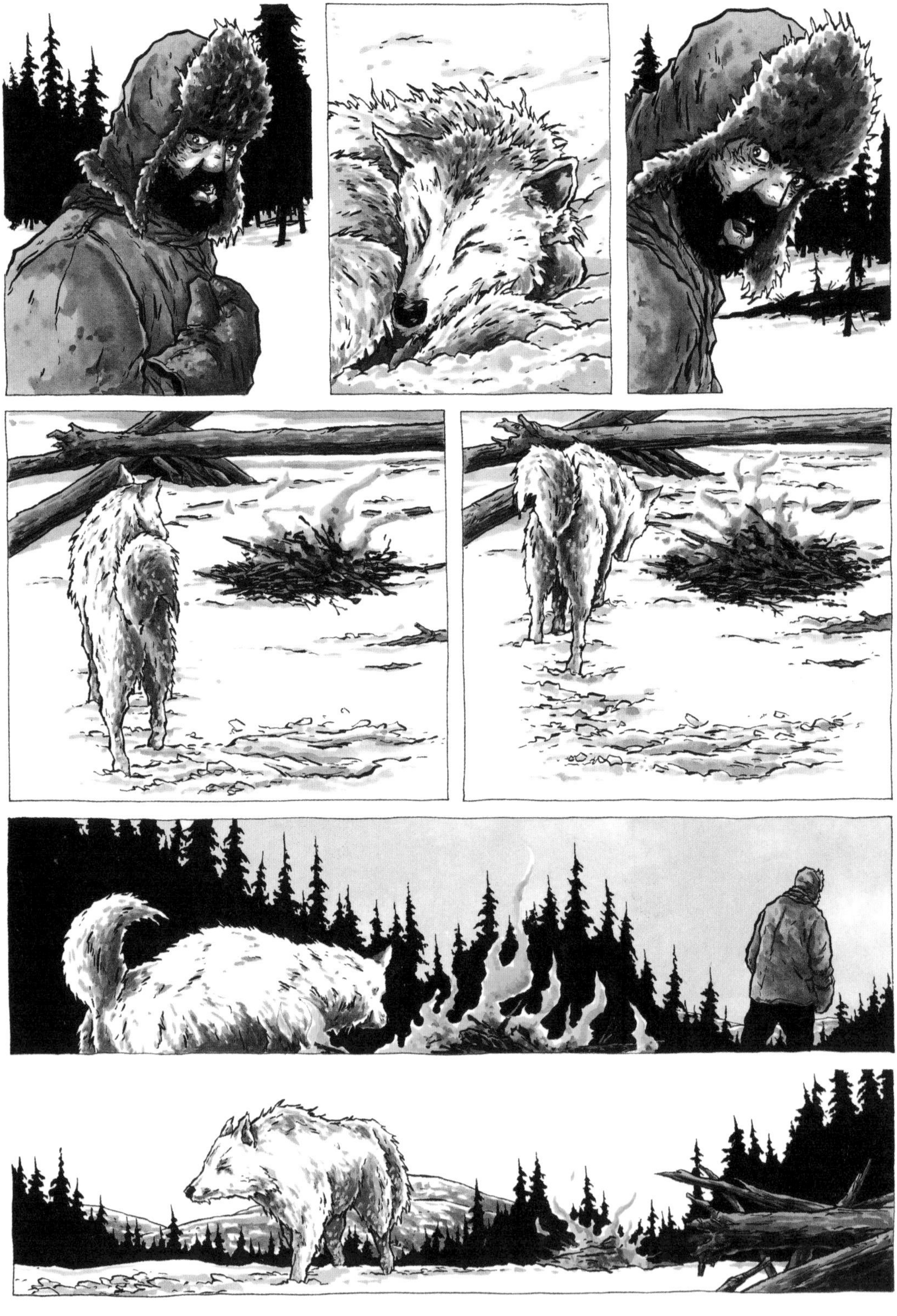

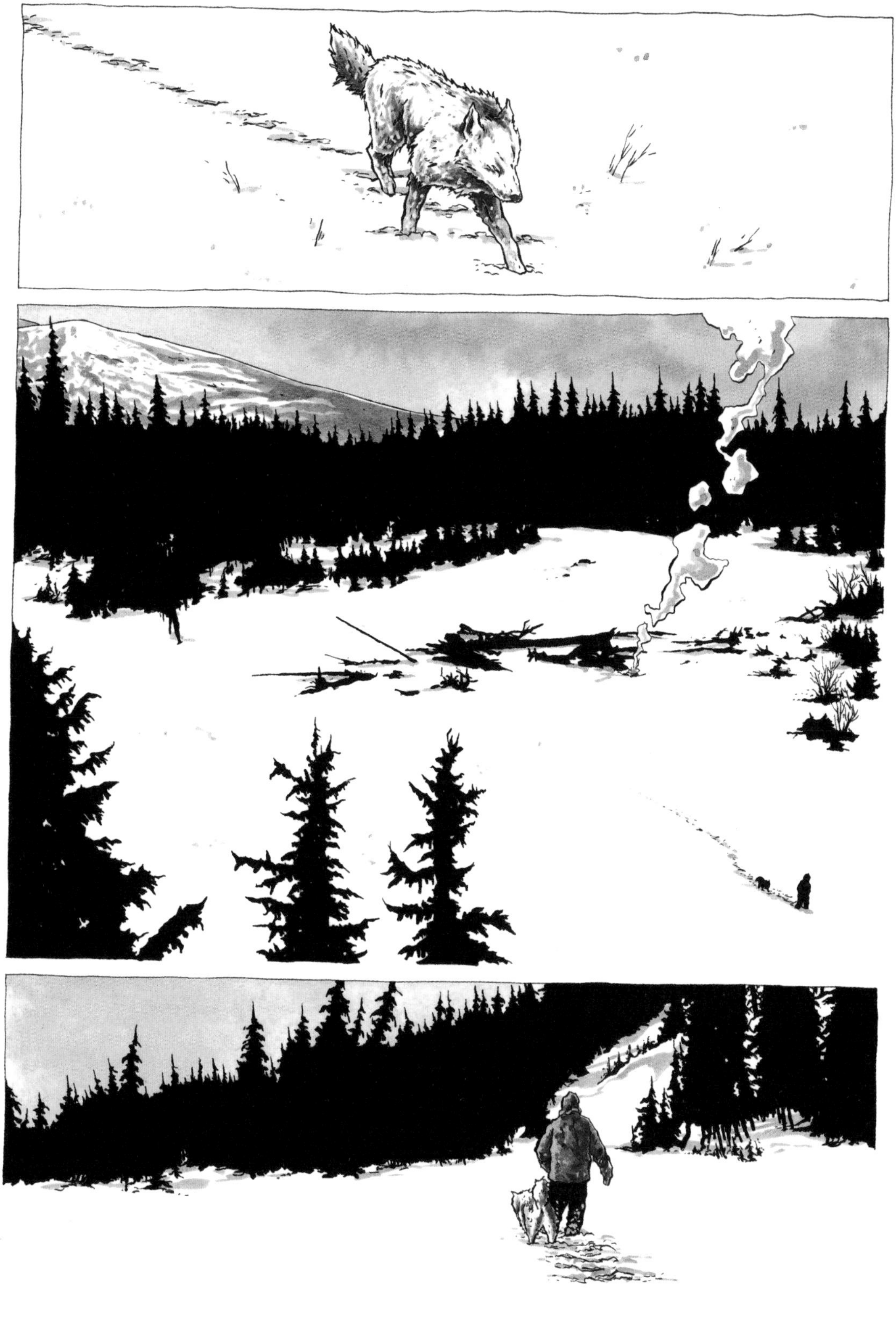

MY POOR
FRIEND . . .

. . . YOU DO
NOT KNOW
COLD . . .

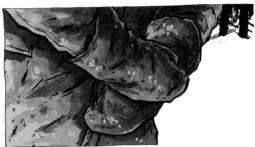

. . . THE
DOG, IT
UNDERSTANDS
. . .

. . . IT
KNOWS
. . .

. . . ALL OF
ITS ANCESTORS
HAVE KNOWN
. . .

. . . AND IT
LISTENS TO
THIS INHERITED
KNOWLEDGE
. . .

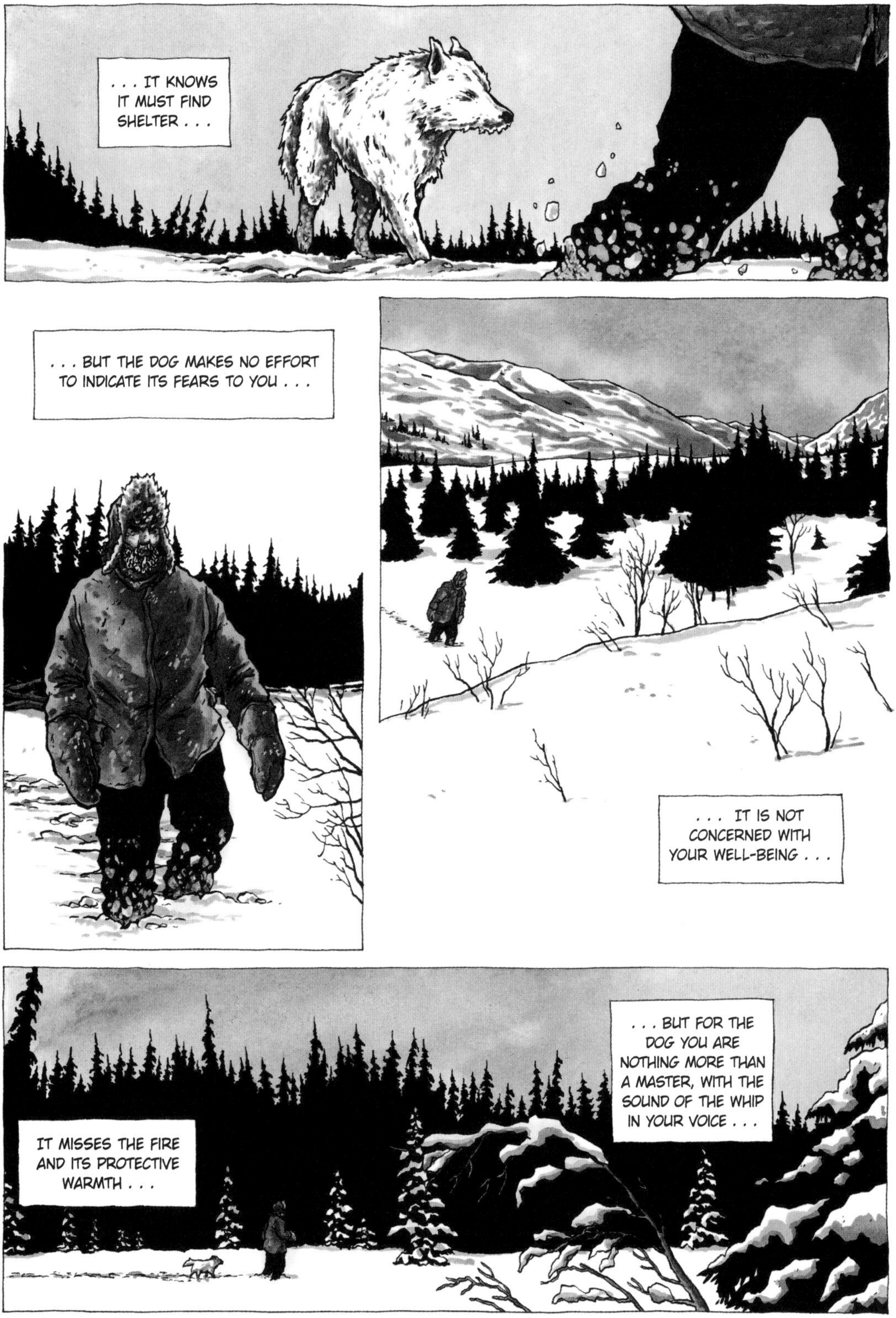
. . . IT KNOWS IT MUST FIND SHELTER . . .
. . . BUT THE DOG MAKES NO EFFORT TO INDICATE ITS FEARS TO YOU . . .
. . . IT IS NOT CONCERNED WITH YOUR WELL-BEING . . .
IT MISSES THE FIRE AND ITS PROTECTIVE WARMTH . . .
. . . BUT FOR THE DOG YOU ARE NOTHING MORE THAN A MASTER, WITH THE SOUND OF THE WHIP IN YOUR VOICE . . .

IT IS THAT, AND ONLY THAT, WHICH MAKES IT FOLLOW YOU . . .

IT SUBMISSIVELY WALKS CLOSE TO YOUR HEELS . . .

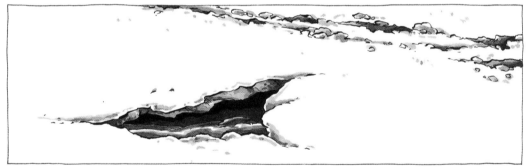

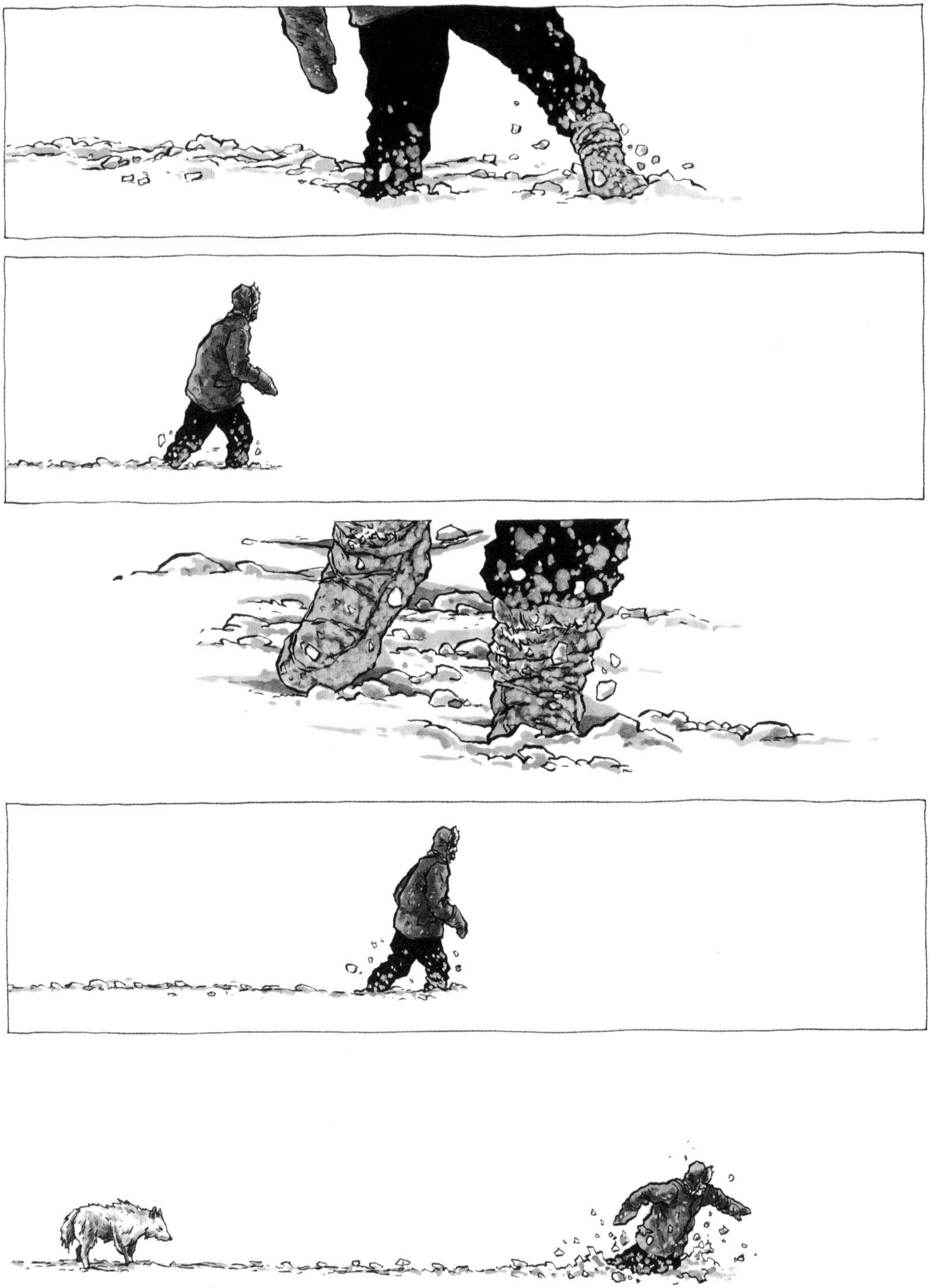

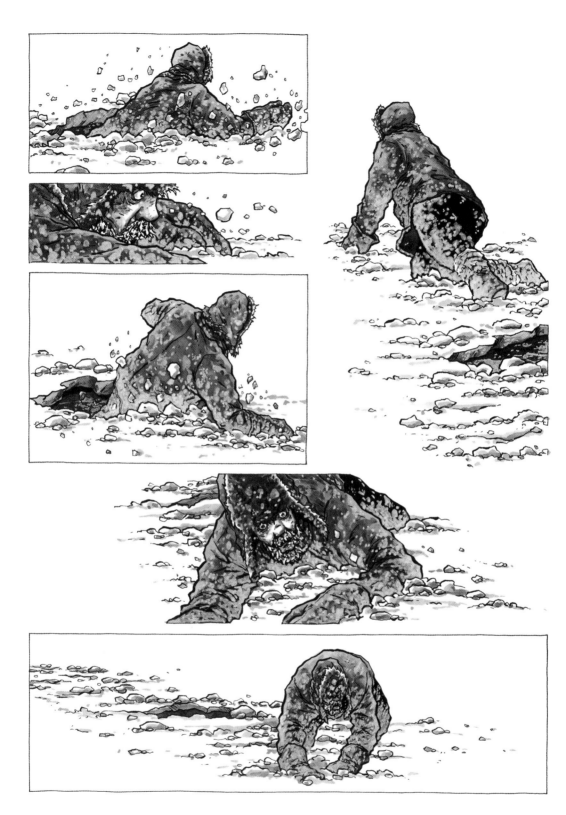

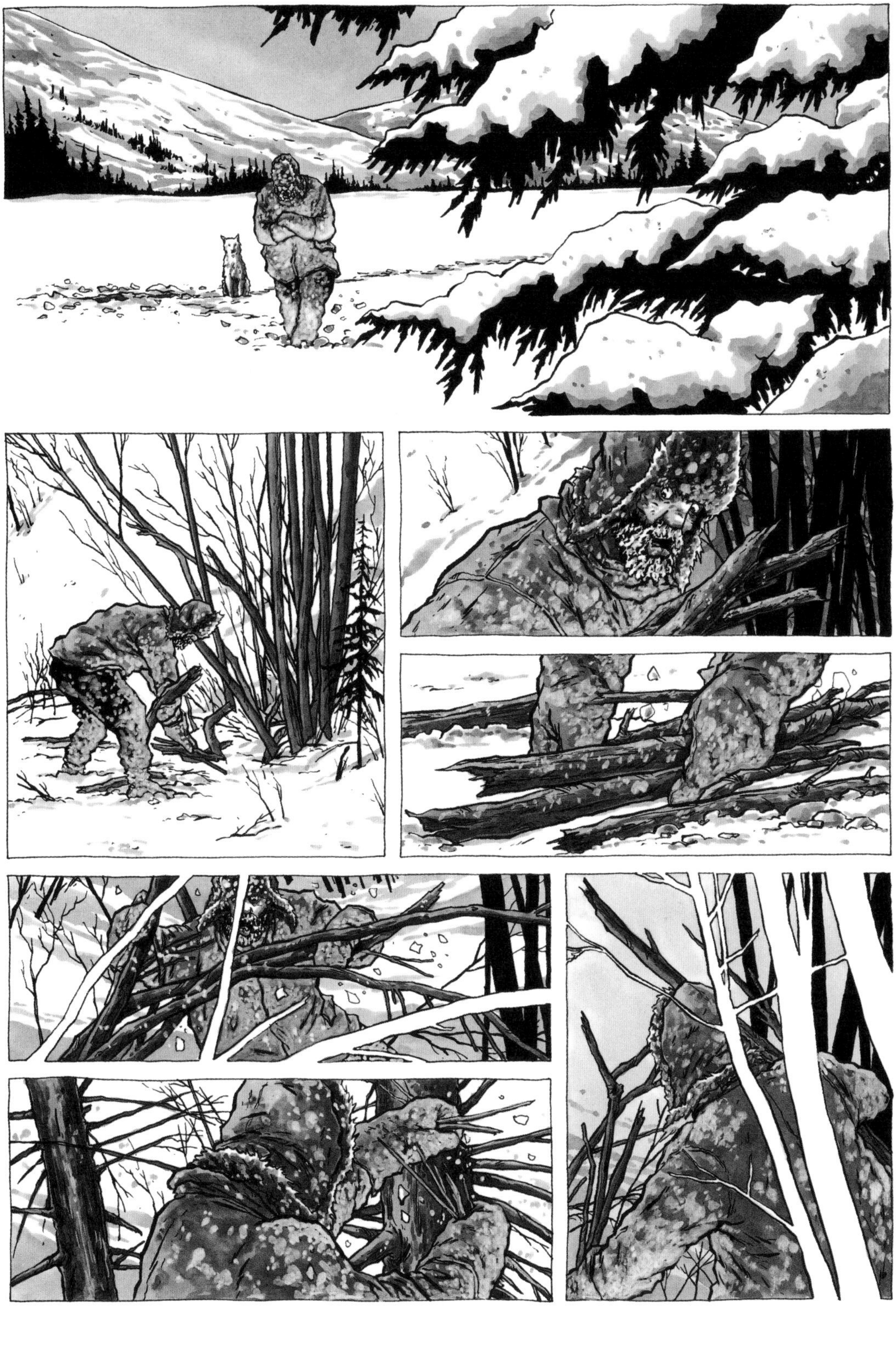

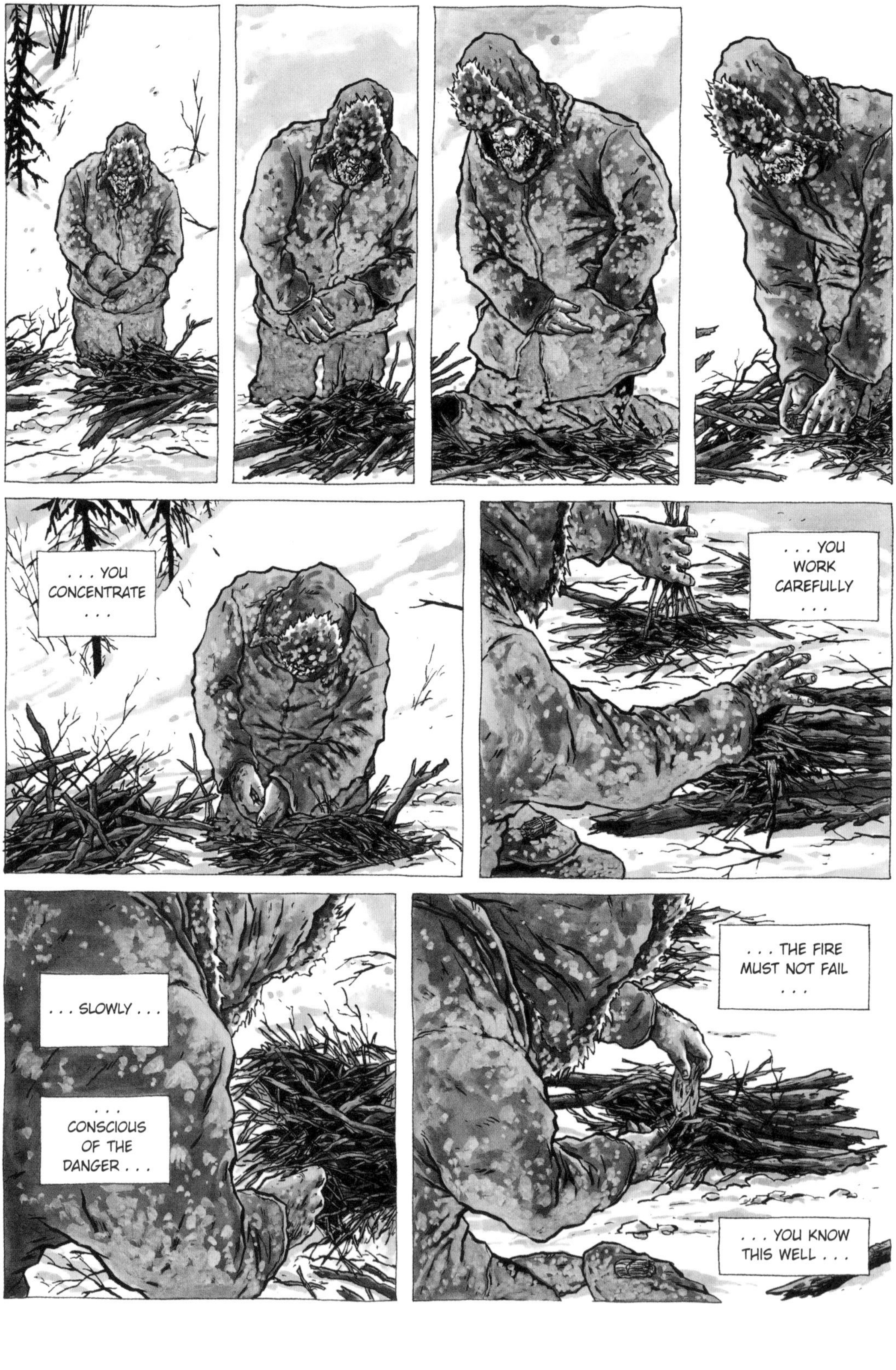
. . . YOU CONCENTRATE . . .
. . . YOU WORK CAREFULLY . . .
. . . SLOWLY . . .
. . . CONSCIOUS OF THE DANGER . . .
. . . THE FIRE MUST NOT FAIL . . .
. . . YOU KNOW THIS WELL . . .

. . . WITH DRY FEET YOU CAN ALWAYS RUN ALONG THE TRAIL HALF A MILE TO KEEP YOUR BLOOD MOVING . . .

. . . BUT YOUR FEET ARE WET AND FREEZING . . .

. . . AND IT IS 75 DEGREES BELOW ZERO . . .

. . . NO MATTER HOW FAST YOU RUN, YOUR WET FEET WILL FREEZE EVEN HARDER . . .

. . . THE OLD MAN ON SULPHUR CREEK TOLD YOU ABOUT IT . . .

. . . NOW YOU ARE GRATEFUL FOR HIS ADVICE . . .

. . . YOU KNOW ALL ABOUT THIS . . .

. . . YOUR FEET HAVE ALREADY LOST ALL FEELING . . .

. . . YOUR FINGERS HAVE ALREADY GONE NUMB . . .

. . . YOUR BLOOD RETREATS INTO THE LOWEST DEPTHS OF YOUR BODY . . .

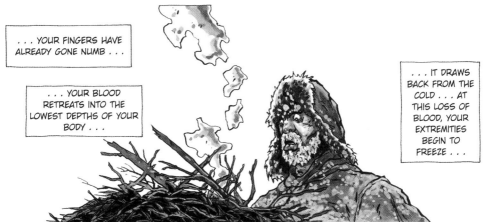

. . . IT DRAWS BACK FROM THE COLD . . . AT THIS LOSS OF BLOOD, YOUR EXTREMITIES BEGIN TO FREEZE . . .

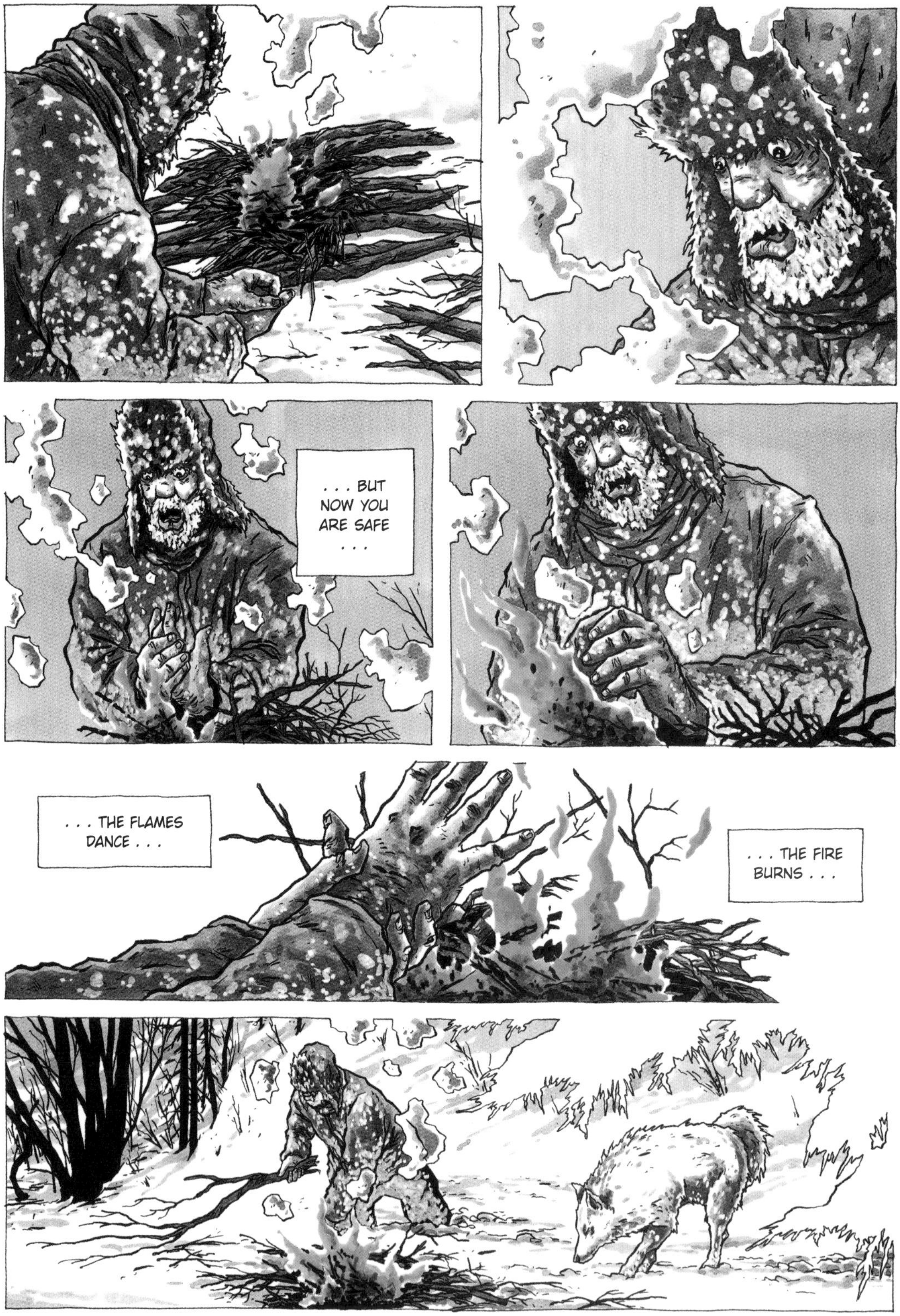
. . . BUT NOW YOU ARE SAFE . . .
. . . THE FLAMES DANCE . . .
. . . THE FIRE BURNS . . .

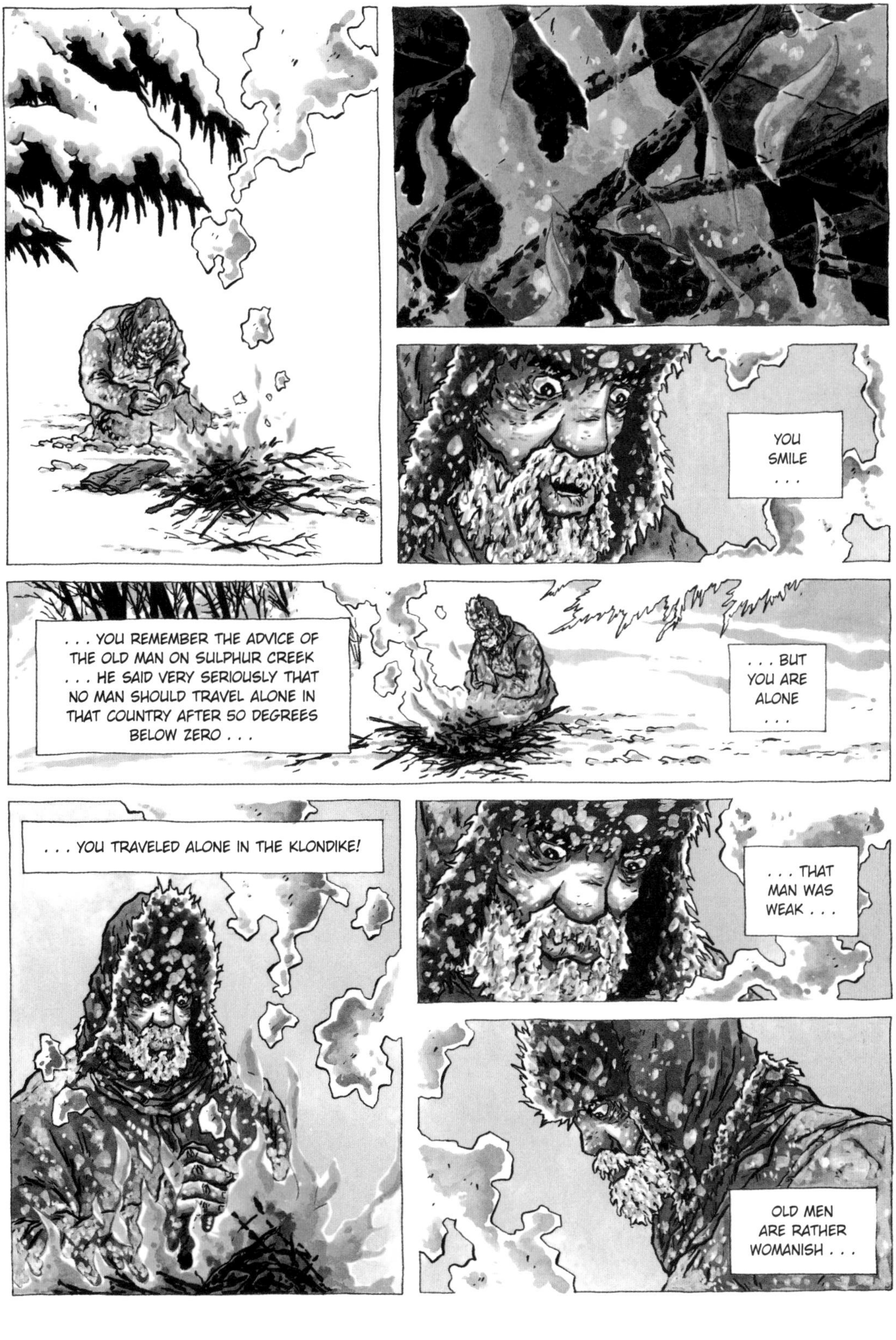
YOU SMILE . . .
. . . YOU REMEMBER THE ADVICE OF THE OLD MAN ON SULPHUR CREEK . . . HE SAID VERY SERIOUSLY THAT NO MAN SHOULD TRAVEL ALONE IN THAT COUNTRY AFTER 50 DEGREES BELOW ZERO . . .
. . . BUT YOU ARE ALONE . . .
. . . YOU TRAVELED ALONE IN THE KLONDIKE!
. . . THAT MAN WAS WEAK . . .
OLD MEN ARE RATHER WOMANISH . . .

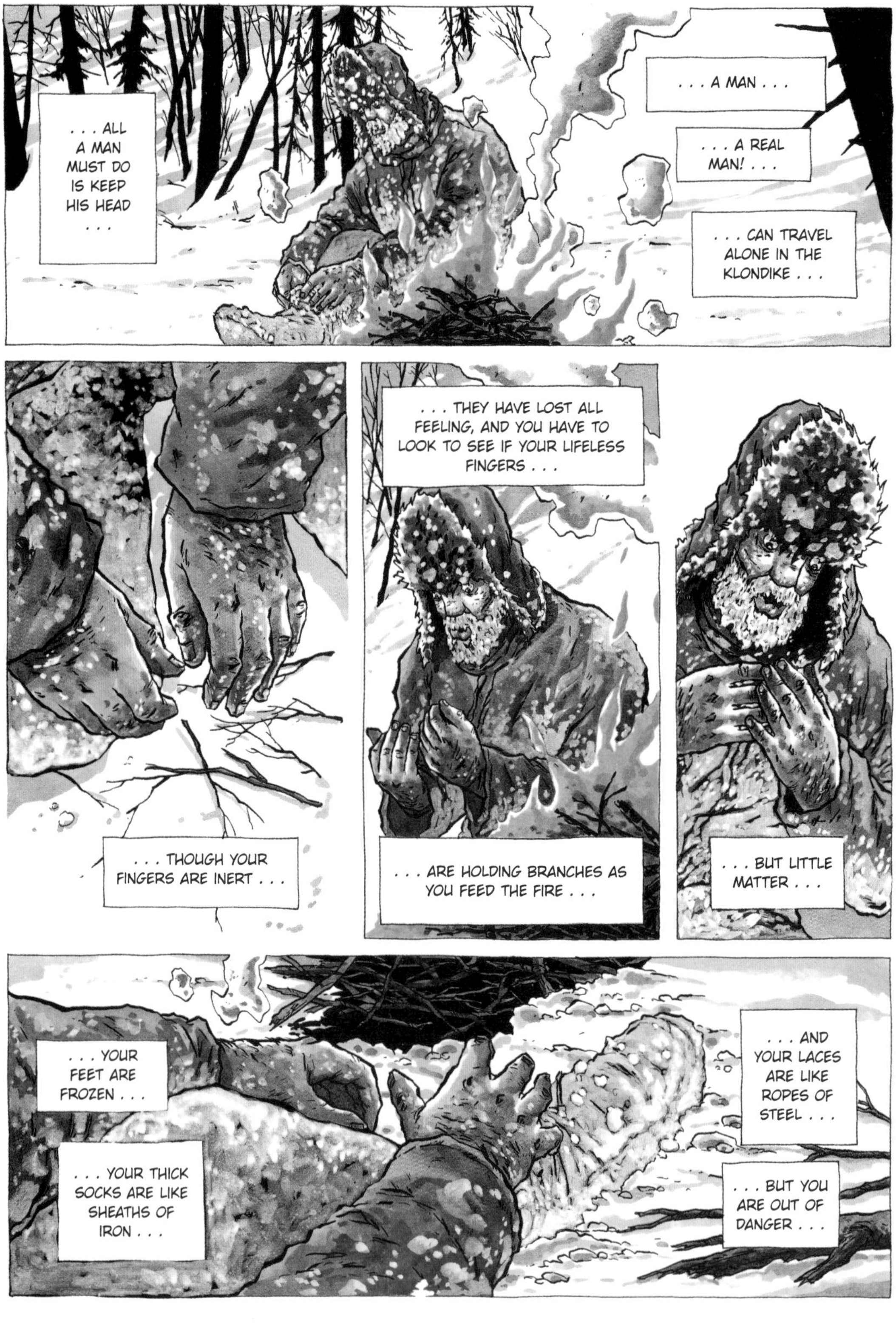
. . . ALL A MAN MUST DO IS KEEP HIS HEAD . . .
. . . A MAN . . .
. . . A REAL MAN! . . .
. . . CAN TRAVEL ALONE IN THE KLONDIKE . . .
. . . THOUGH YOUR FINGERS ARE INERT . . .
. . . THEY HAVE LOST ALL FEELING, AND YOU HAVE TO LOOK TO SEE IF YOUR LIFELESS FINGERS . . .
. . . ARE HOLDING BRANCHES AS YOU FEED THE FIRE . . .
. . . BUT LITTLE MATTER . . .
. . . YOUR FEET ARE FROZEN . . .
. . . YOUR THICK SOCKS ARE LIKE SHEATHS OF IRON . . .
. . . AND YOUR LACES ARE LIKE ROPES OF STEEL . . .
. . . BUT YOU ARE OUT OF DANGER . . .

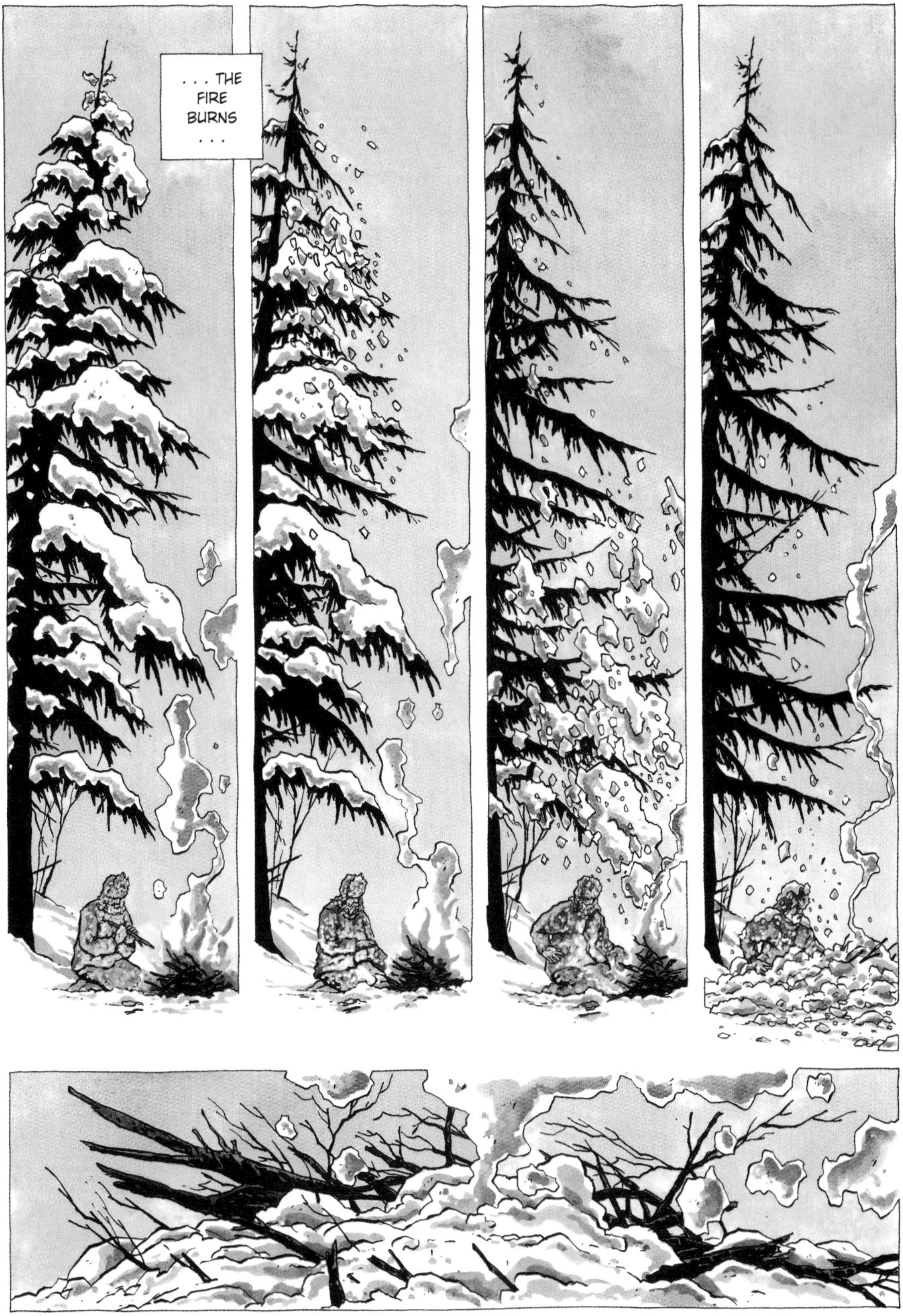
. . . THE FIRE BURNS . . .

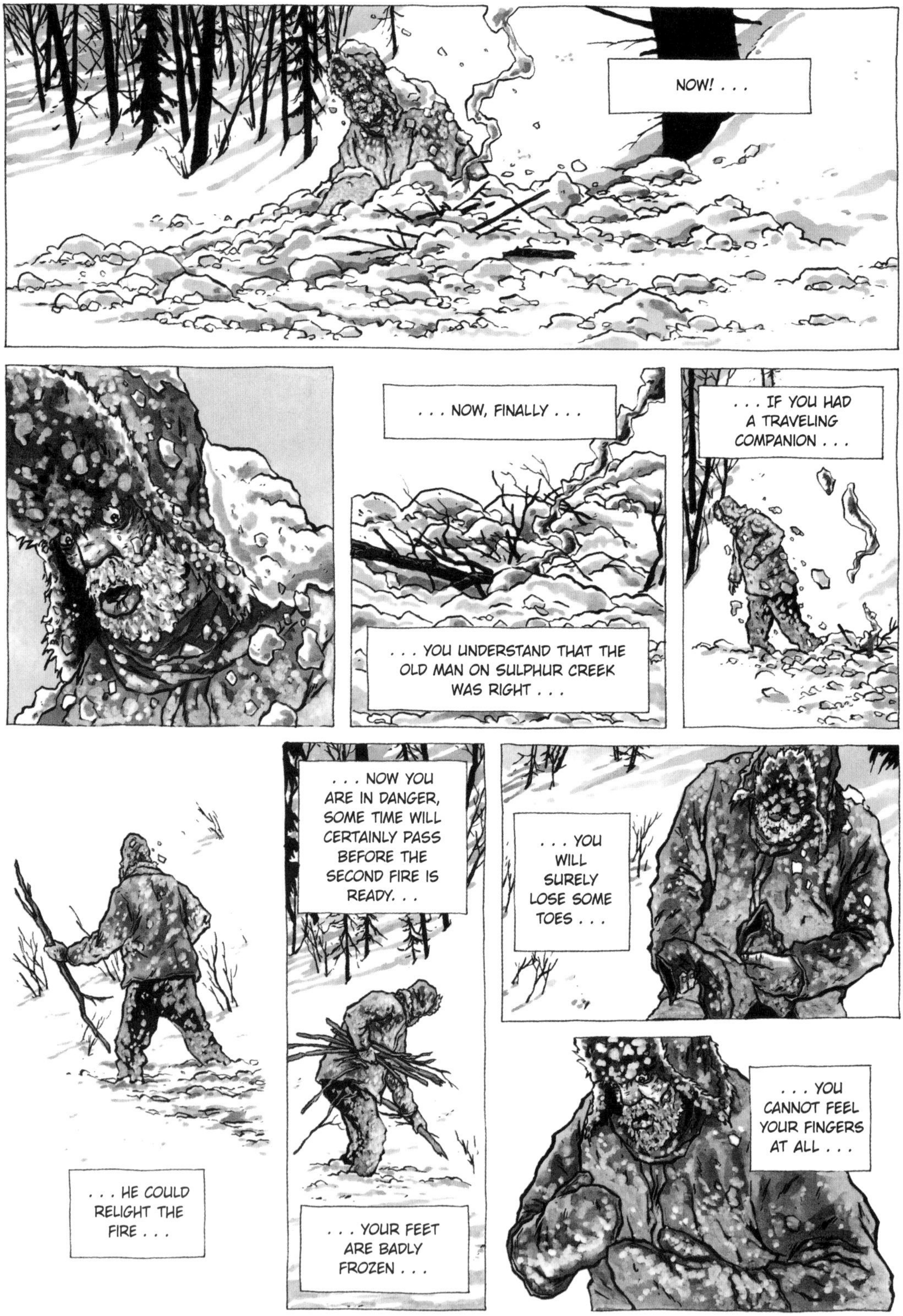
NOW! . . .
. . . NOW, FINALLY . . .
. . . YOU UNDERSTAND THAT THE OLD MAN ON SULPHUR CREEK WAS RIGHT . . .
. . . IF YOU HAD A TRAVELING COMPANION . . .
. . . HE COULD RELIGHT THE FIRE . . .
. . . NOW YOU ARE IN DANGER, SOME TIME WILL CERTAINLY PASS BEFORE THE SECOND FIRE IS READY. . .
. . . YOUR FEET ARE BADLY FROZEN . . .
. . . YOU WILL SURELY LOSE SOME TOES . . .
. . . YOU CANNOT FEEL YOUR FINGERS AT ALL . . .

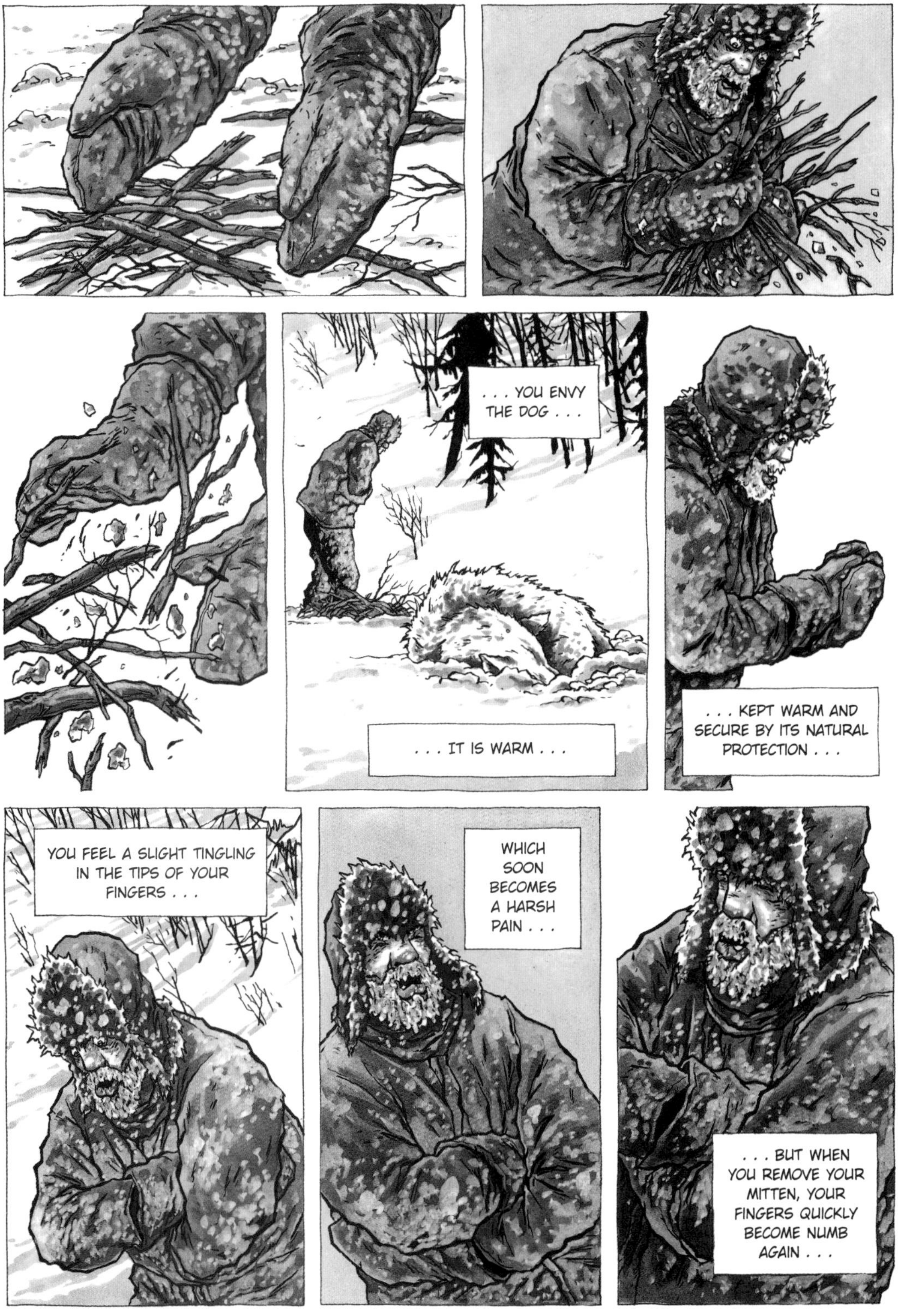
. . . YOU ENVY THE DOG . . .
. . . IT IS WARM . . .
. . . KEPT WARM AND SECURE BY ITS NATURAL PROTECTION . . .
YOU FEEL A SLIGHT TINGLING IN THE TIPS OF YOUR FINGERS . . .
WHICH SOON BECOMES A HARSH PAIN . . .
. . . BUT WHEN YOU REMOVE YOUR MITTEN, YOUR FINGERS QUICKLY BECOME NUMB AGAIN . . .

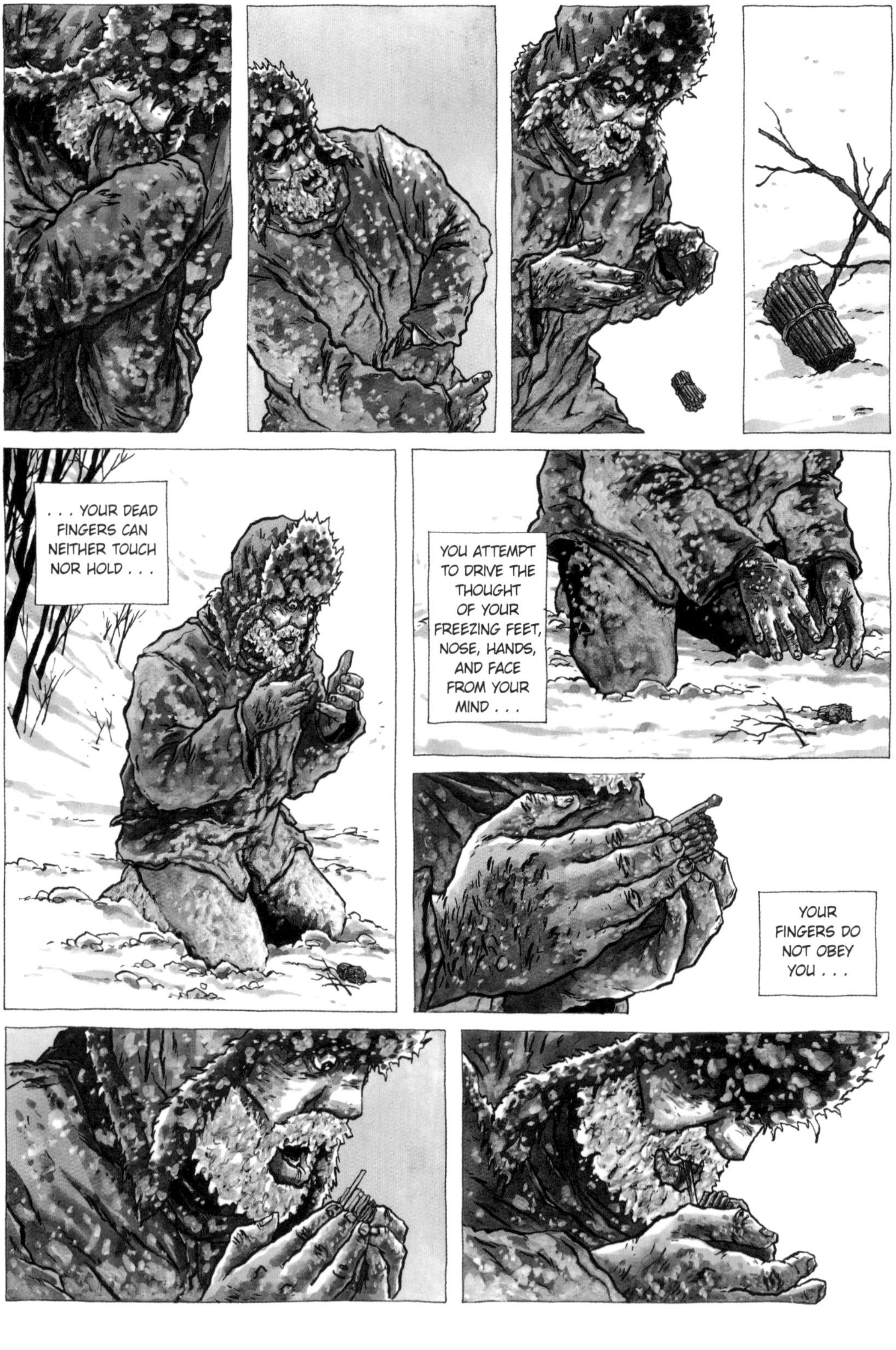
. . . YOUR DEAD FINGERS CAN NEITHER TOUCH NOR HOLD . . .
YOU ATTEMPT TO DRIVE THE THOUGHT OF YOUR FREEZING FEET, NOSE, HANDS, AND FACE FROM YOUR MIND . . .
YOUR FINGERS DO NOT OBEY YOU . . .

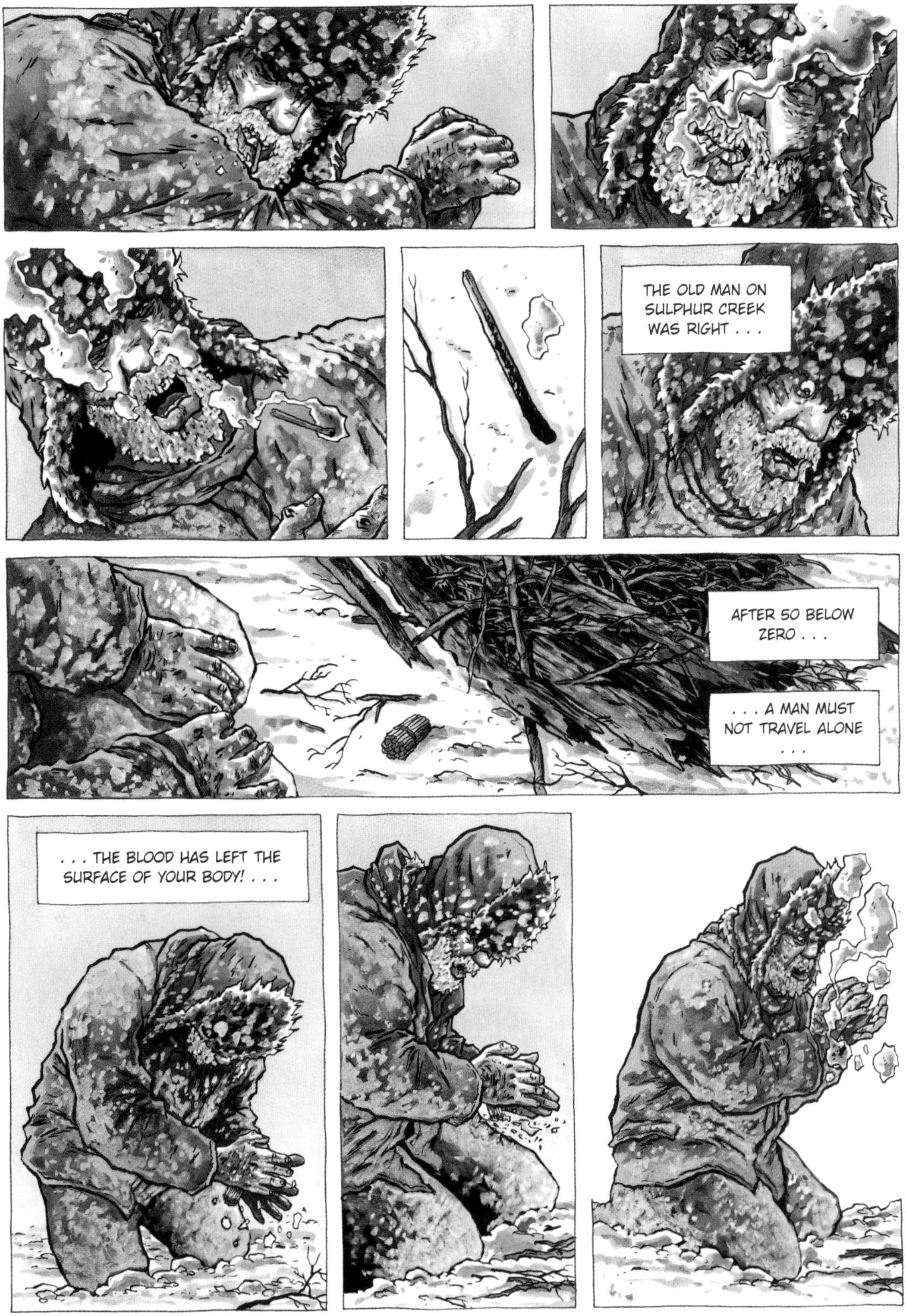
THE OLD MAN ON SULPHUR CREEK WAS RIGHT . . .
AFTER 50 BELOW ZERO . . .
. . . A MAN MUST NOT TRAVEL ALONE . . .
. . . THE BLOOD HAS LEFT THE SURFACE OF YOUR BODY! . . .

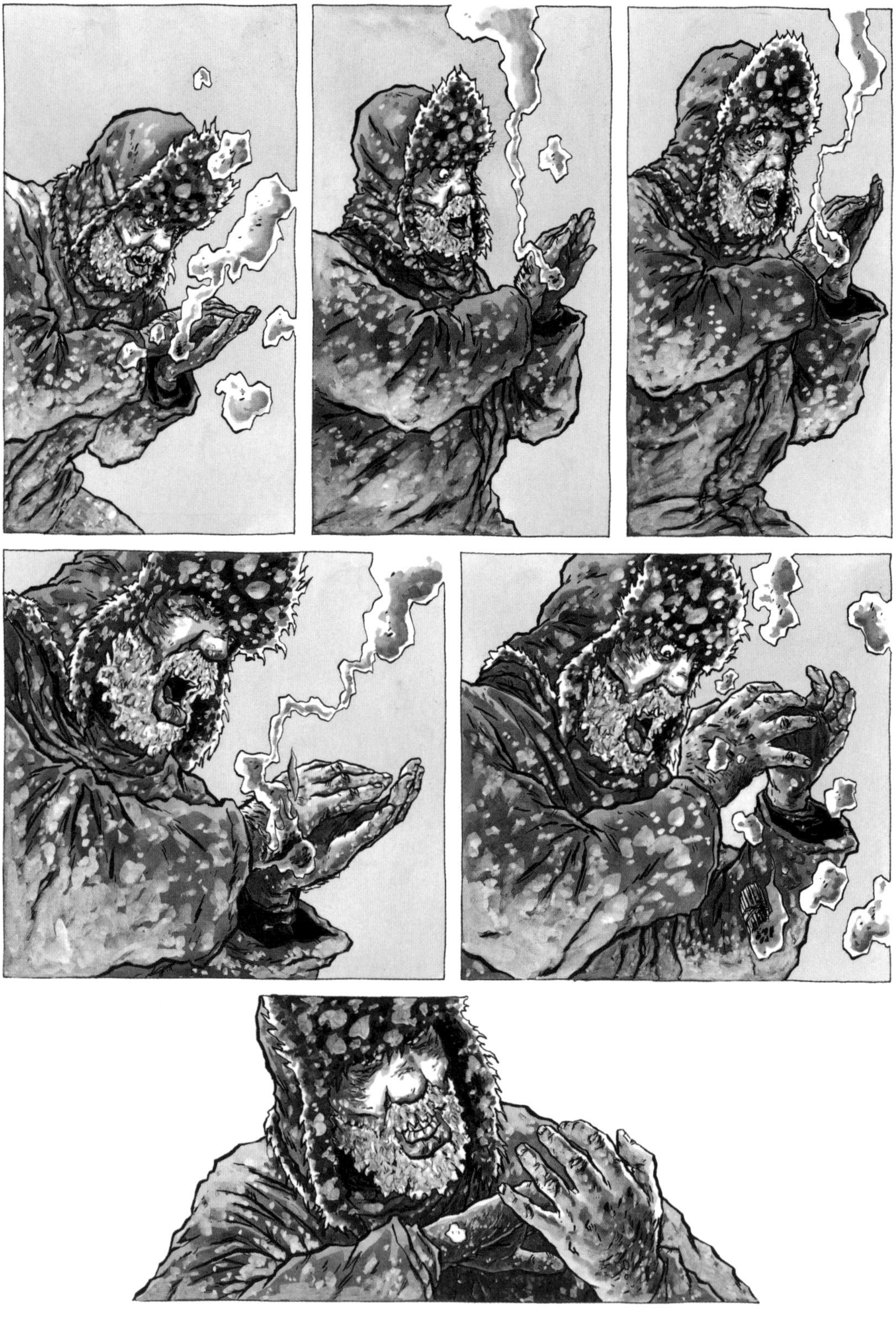

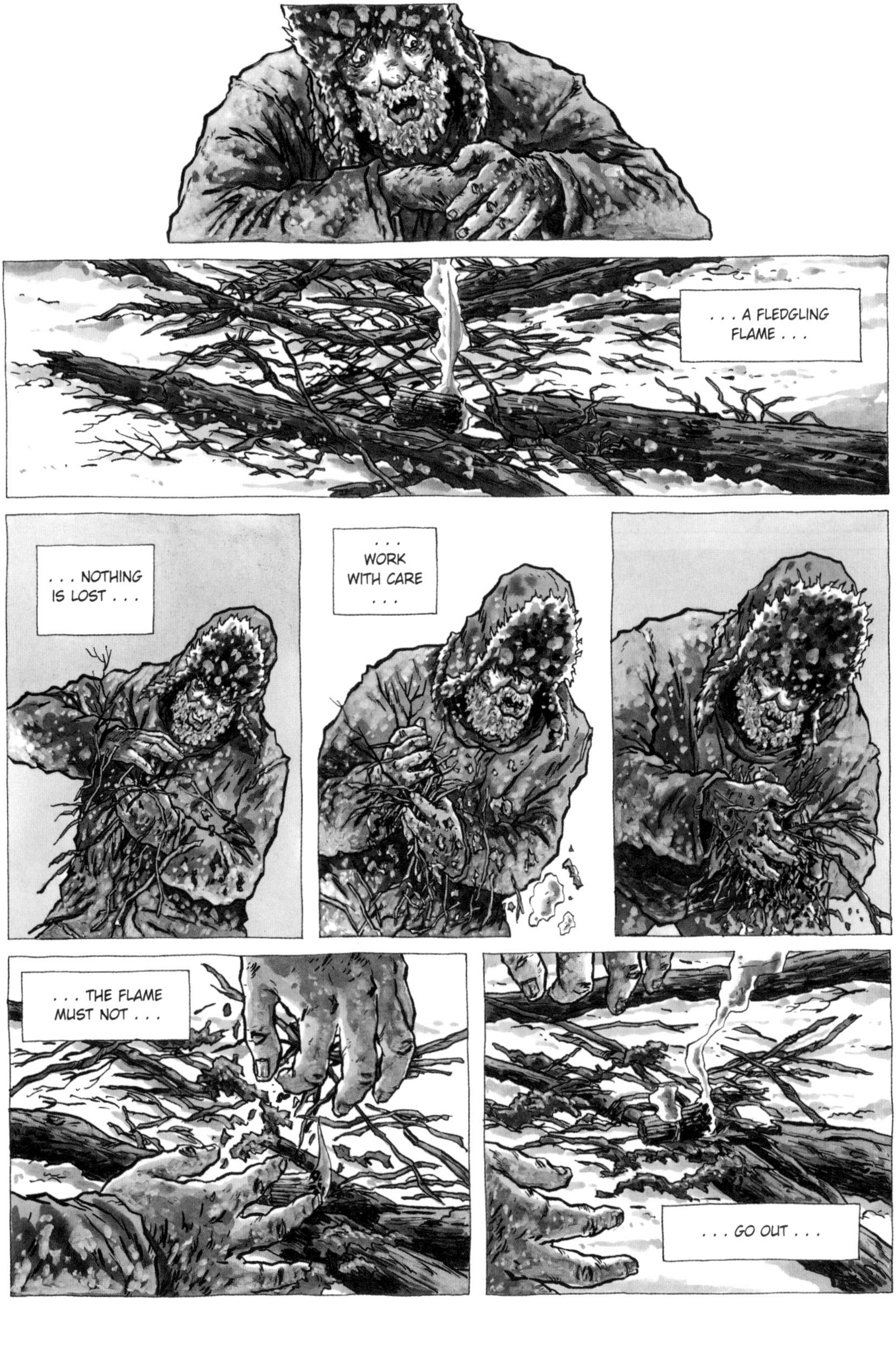
. . . A FLEDGLING FLAME . . .
. . . NOTHING IS LOST . . .
. . . WORK WITH CARE . . .
. . . THE FLAME MUST NOT . . .
. . . GO OUT . . .

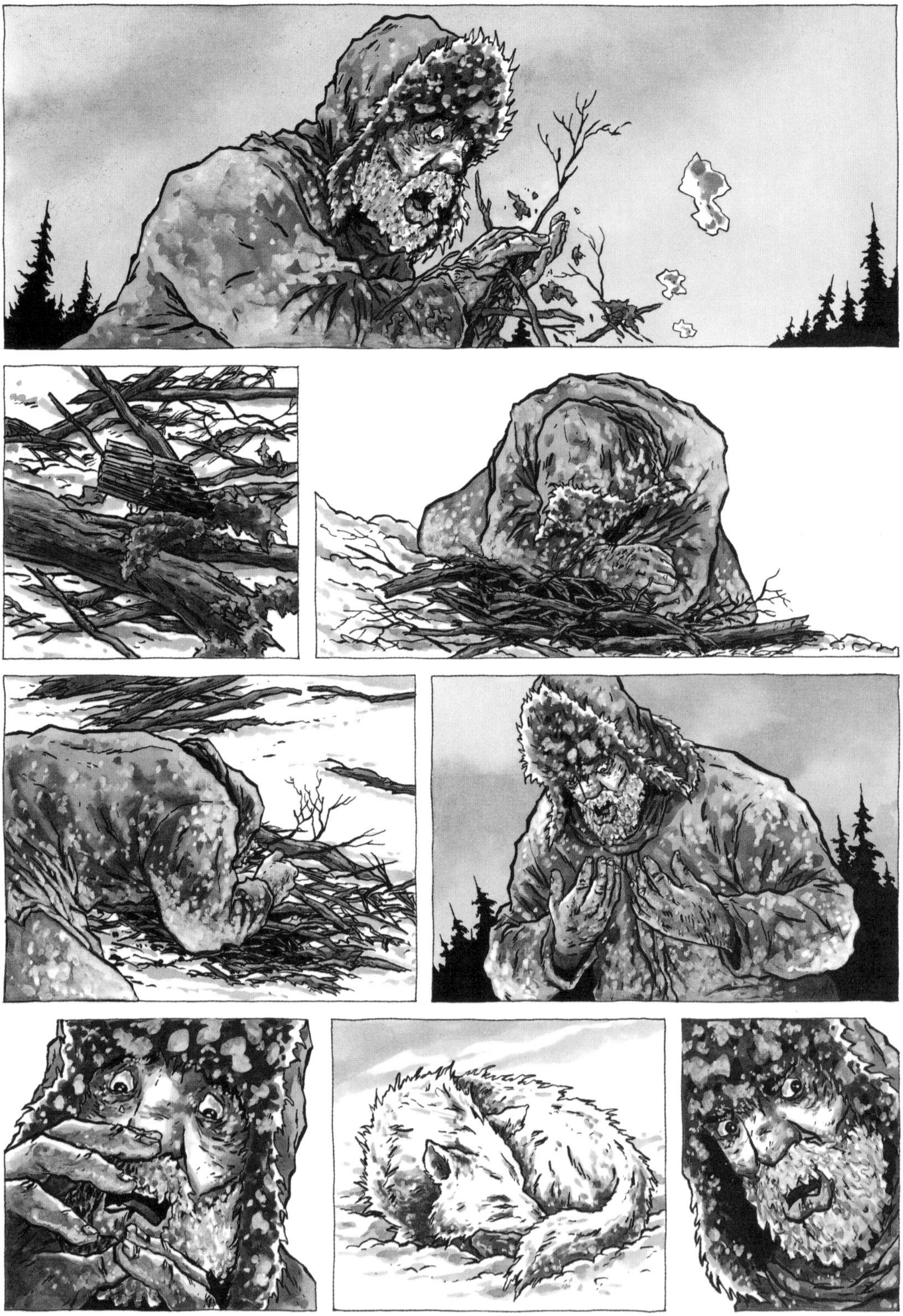

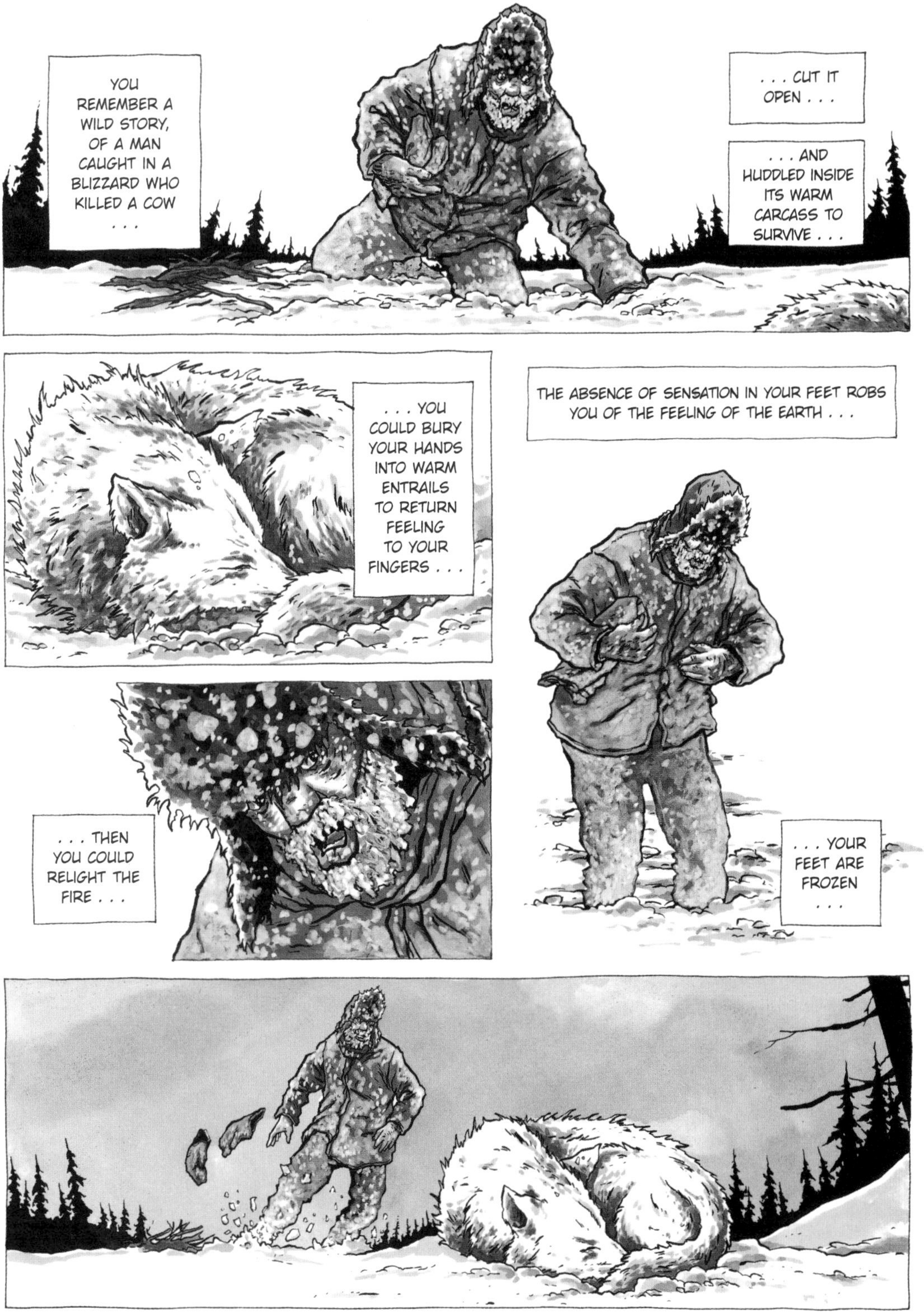
YOU REMEMBER A WILD STORY, OF A MAN CAUGHT IN A BLIZZARD WHO KILLED A COW . . .
. . . CUT IT OPEN . . .
. . . AND HUDDLED INSIDE ITS WARM CARCASS TO SURVIVE . . .
. . . YOU COULD BURY YOUR HANDS INTO WARM ENTRAILS TO RETURN FEELING TO YOUR FINGERS . . .
. . . THEN YOU COULD RELIGHT THE FIRE . . .
THE ABSENCE OF SENSATION IN YOUR FEET ROBS YOU OF THE FEELING OF THE EARTH . . .
. . . YOUR FEET ARE FROZEN . . .

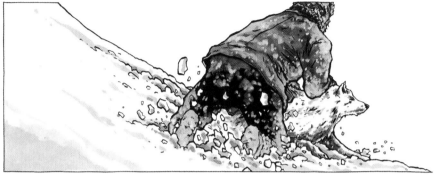

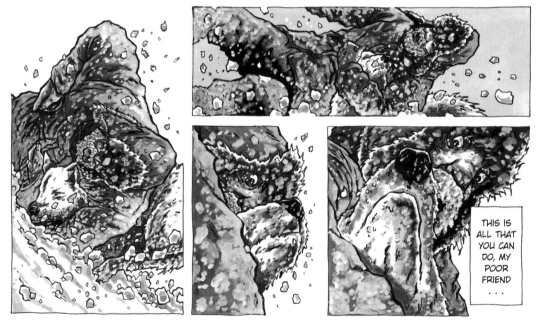

THIS IS ALL THAT YOU CAN DO, MY POOR FRIEND . . .

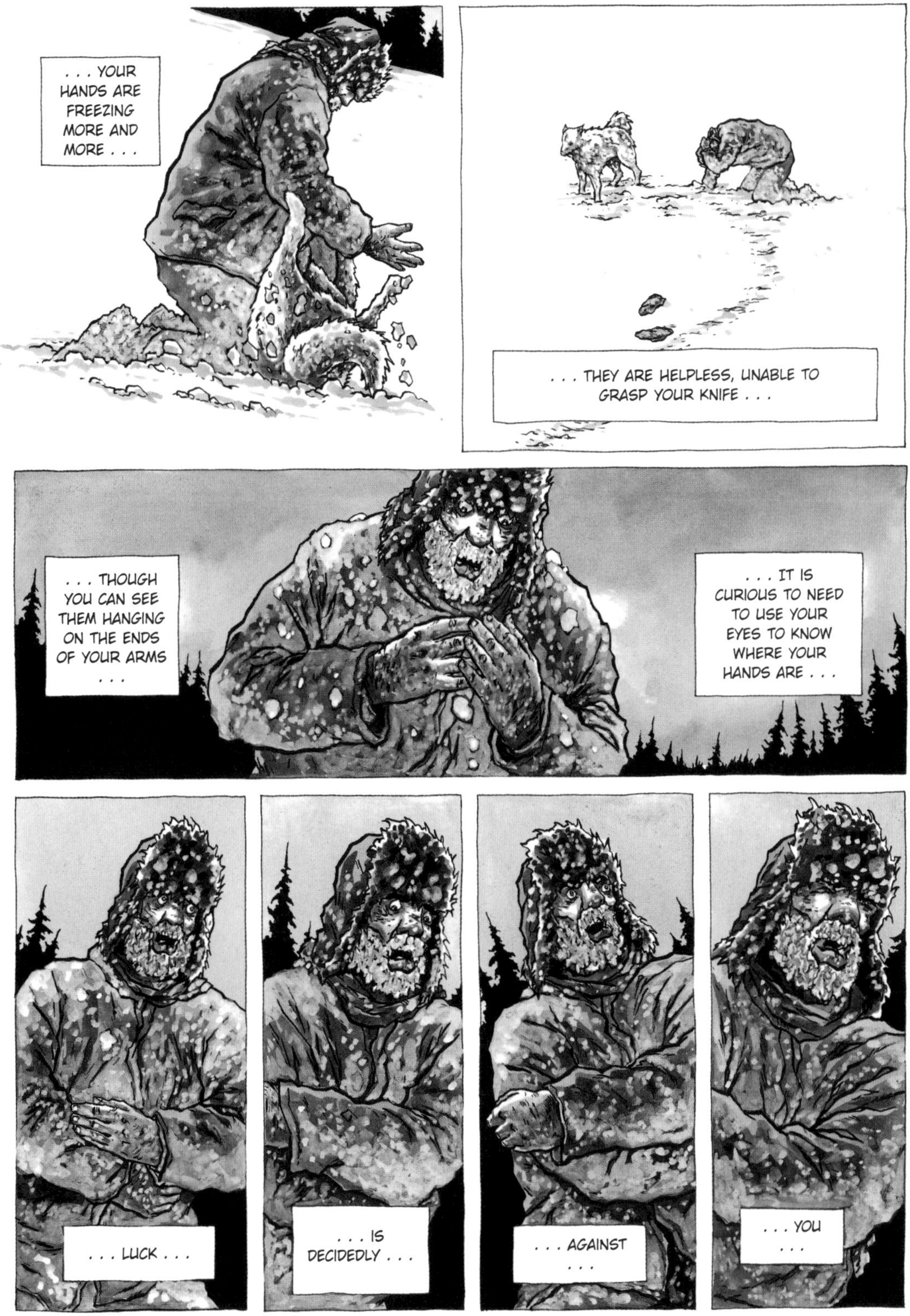
. . . YOUR HANDS ARE FREEZING MORE AND MORE . . .
. . . THEY ARE HELPLESS, UNABLE TO GRASP YOUR KNIFE . . .
. . . THOUGH YOU CAN SEE THEM HANGING ON THE ENDS OF YOUR ARMS . . .
. . . IT IS CURIOUS TO NEED TO USE YOUR EYES TO KNOW WHERE YOUR HANDS ARE . . .
. . . LUCK . . .
. . . IS DECIDEDLY . . .
. . . AGAINST . . .
. . . YOU . . .

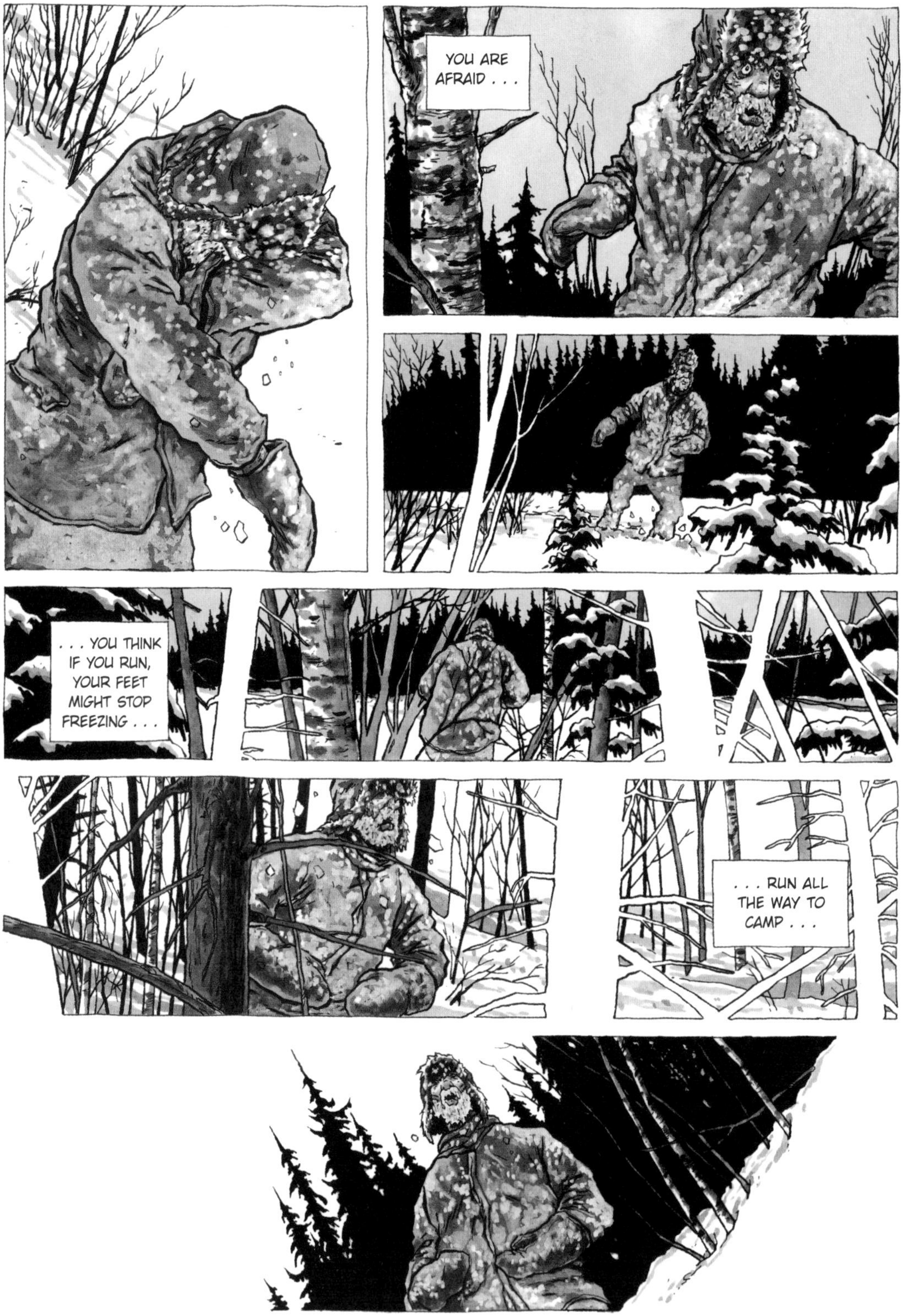
YOU ARE AFRAID . . .
. . . YOU THINK IF YOU RUN, YOUR FEET MIGHT STOP FREEZING . . .
. . . RUN ALL THE WAY TO CAMP . . .

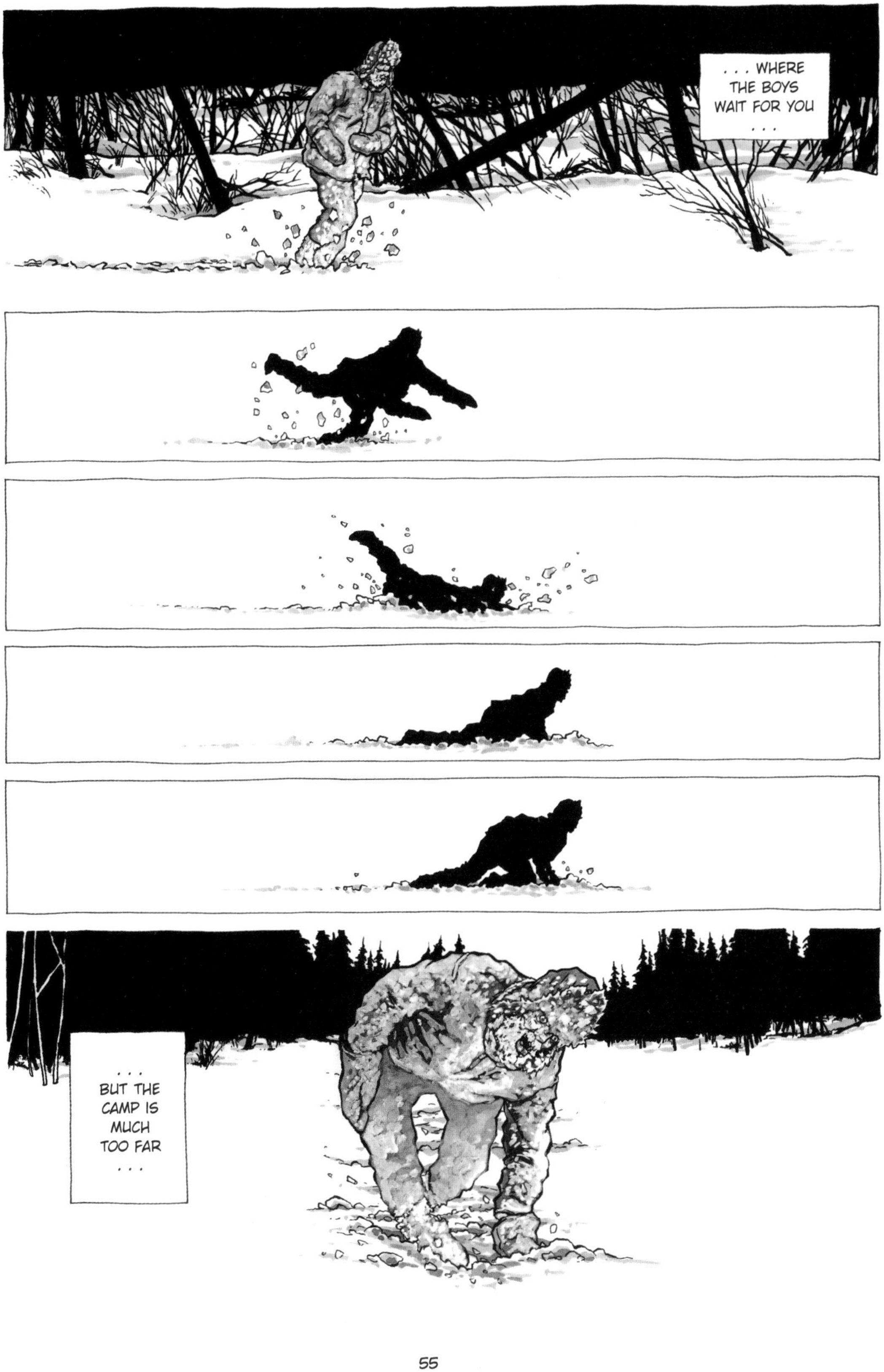
. . . WHERE THE BOYS WAIT FOR YOU . . .
. . . BUT THE CAMP IS MUCH TOO FAR . . .

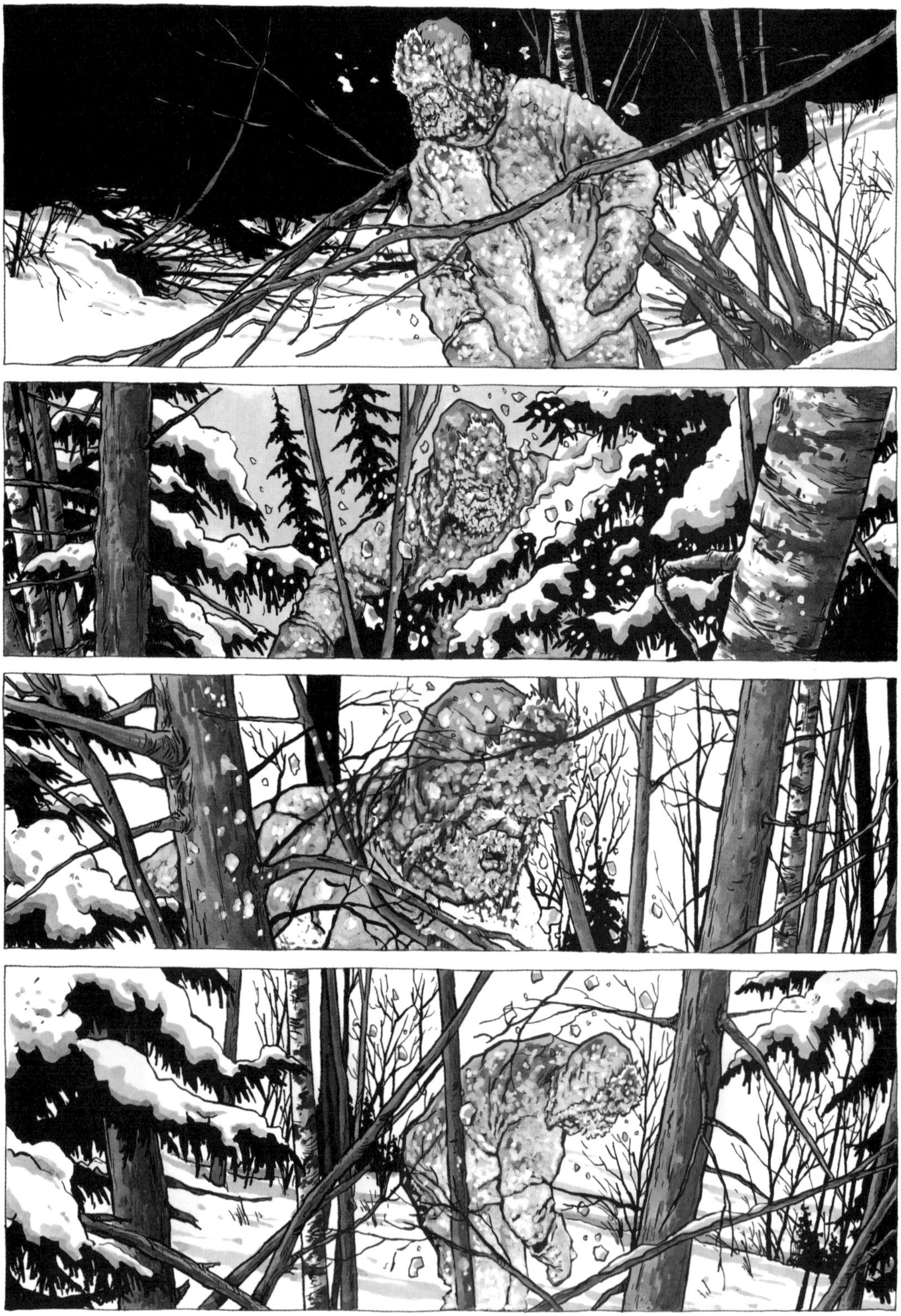

. . . THE COLD HAS TOO GREAT A HEAD START . . .

. . . AND YOU LACK THE ENDURANCE . . .

. . . YOU DO NOT FEEL YOUR FEET TOUCH THE GROUND . . .

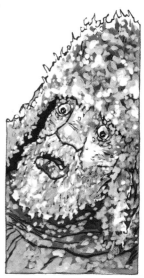

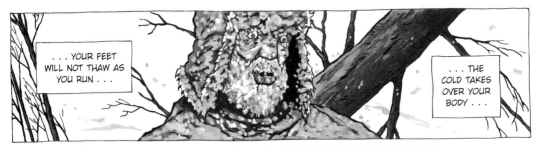

. . . YOUR FEET WILL NOT THAW AS YOU RUN . . .

. . . THE COLD TAKES OVER YOUR BODY . . .

YOU HAVE BEEN ACTING A FOOL, RUNNING AROUND LIKE A CHICKEN WITH ITS HEAD CUT OFF . . .

. . . YOU ARE CERTAIN TO FREEZE . . .

. . . HE REALLY WAS RIGHT, THE OLD MAN ON SULPHUR CREEK . . .

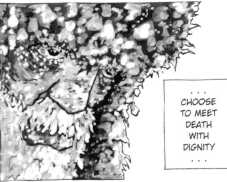

. . . CHOOSE TO MEET DEATH WITH DIGNITY . . .

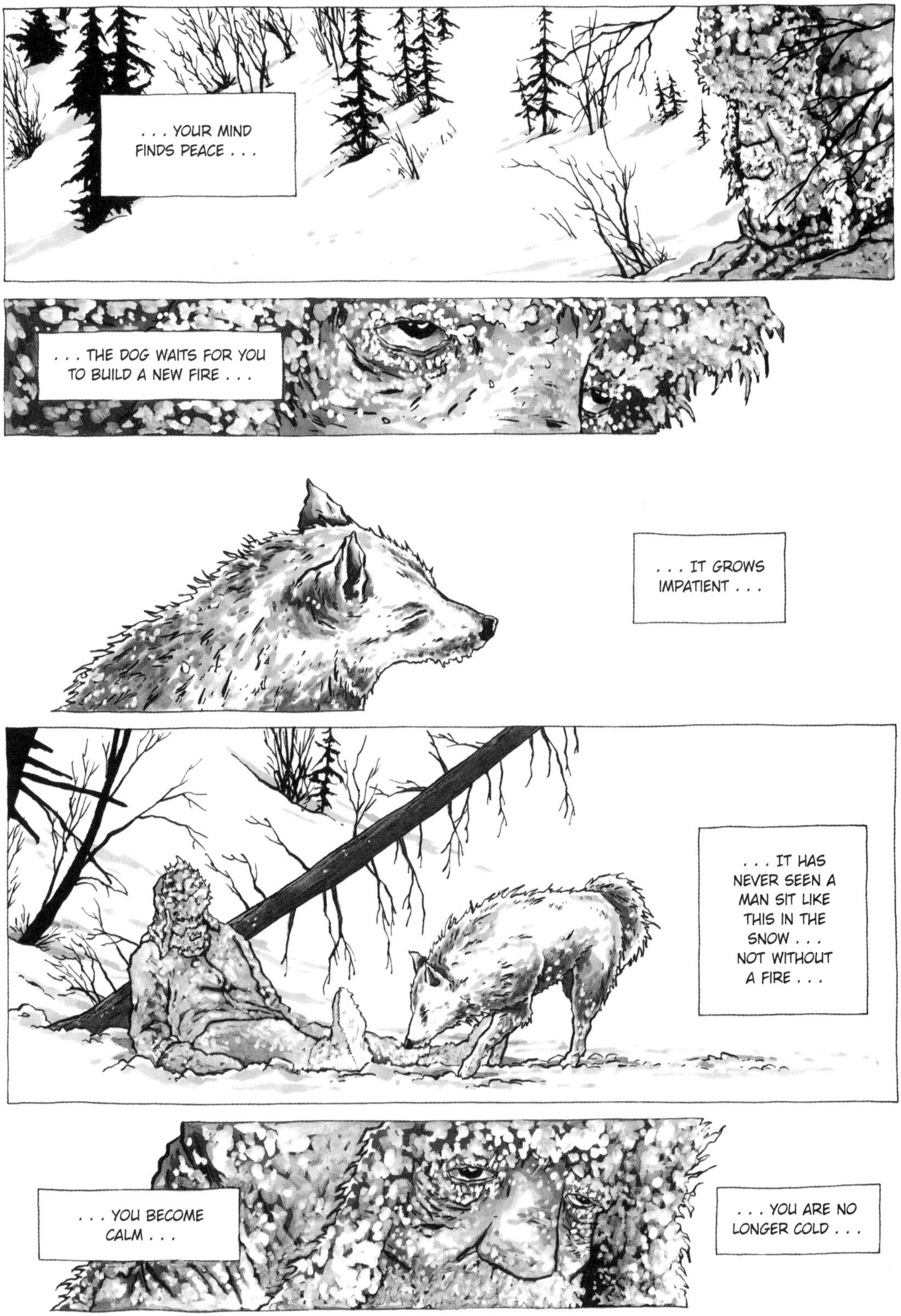

. . . YOUR MIND FINDS PEACE . . .
. . . THE DOG WAITS FOR YOU TO BUILD A NEW FIRE . . .
. . . IT GROWS IMPATIENT . . .
. . . IT HAS NEVER SEEN A MAN SIT LIKE THIS IN THE SNOW . . . NOT WITHOUT A FIRE . . .
. . . YOU BECOME CALM . . .
. . . YOU ARE NO LONGER COLD . . .

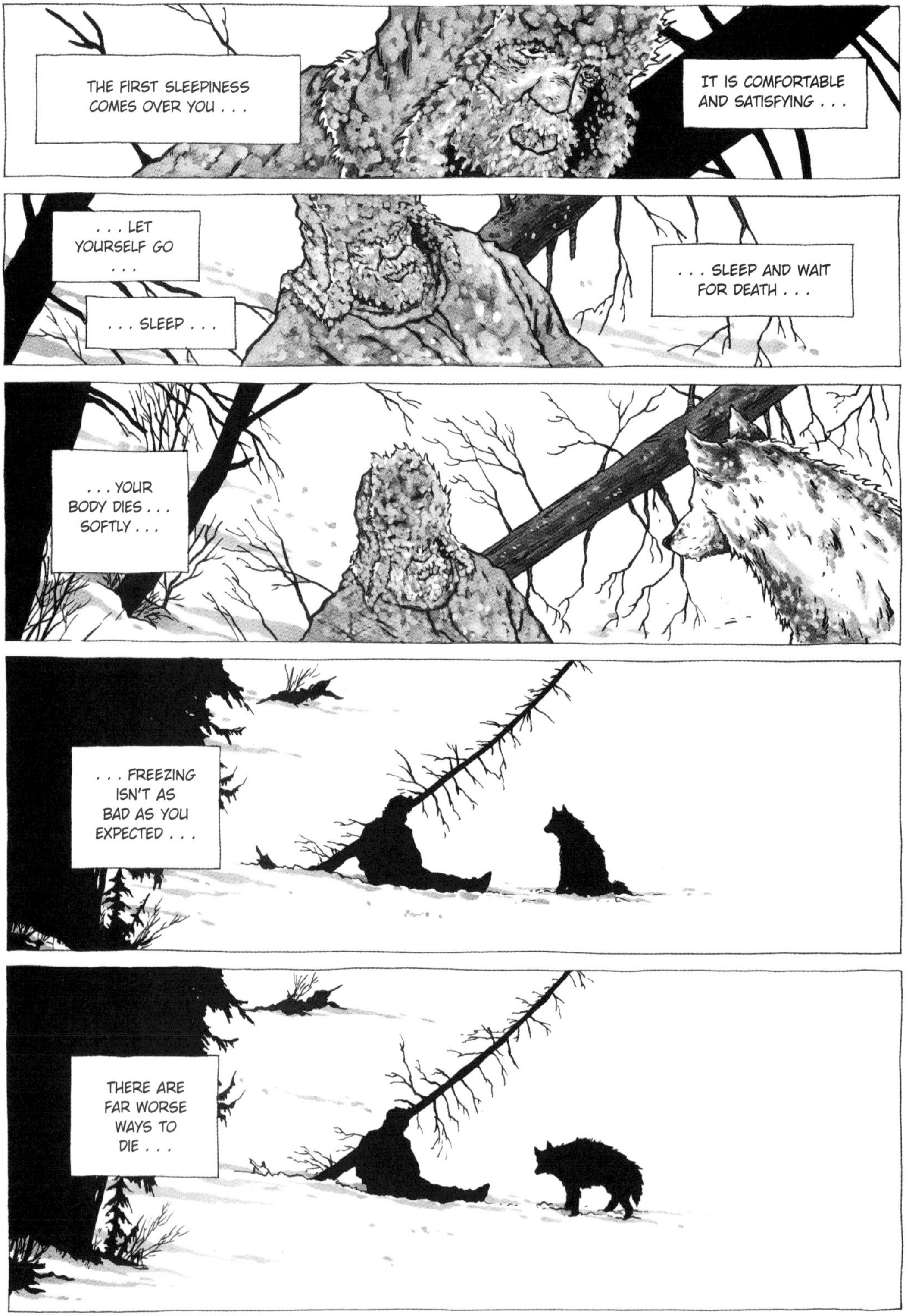
THE FIRST SLEEPINESS COMES OVER YOU . . .
IT IS COMFORTABLE AND SATISFYING . . .
. . . LET YOURSELF GO . . .
. . . SLEEP . . .
. . . SLEEP AND WAIT FOR DEATH . . .
. . . YOUR BODY DIES . . . SOFTLY . . .
. . . FREEZING ISN'T AS BAD AS YOU EXPECTED . . .
THERE ARE FAR WORSE WAYS TO DIE . . .

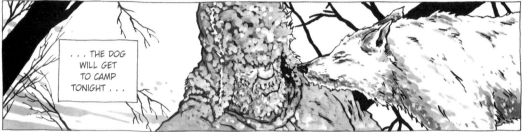

. . . THE DOG
WILL GET
TO CAMP
TONIGHT . . .

. . . WHERE THERE
WILL BE FOOD . . .

. . . AND WHERE
IT WILL FIND . . .

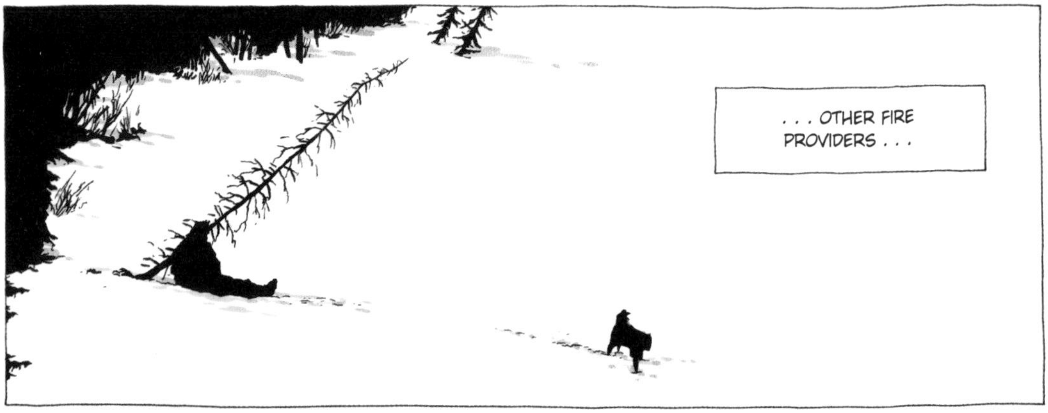
. . . OTHER FIRE PROVIDERS . . .

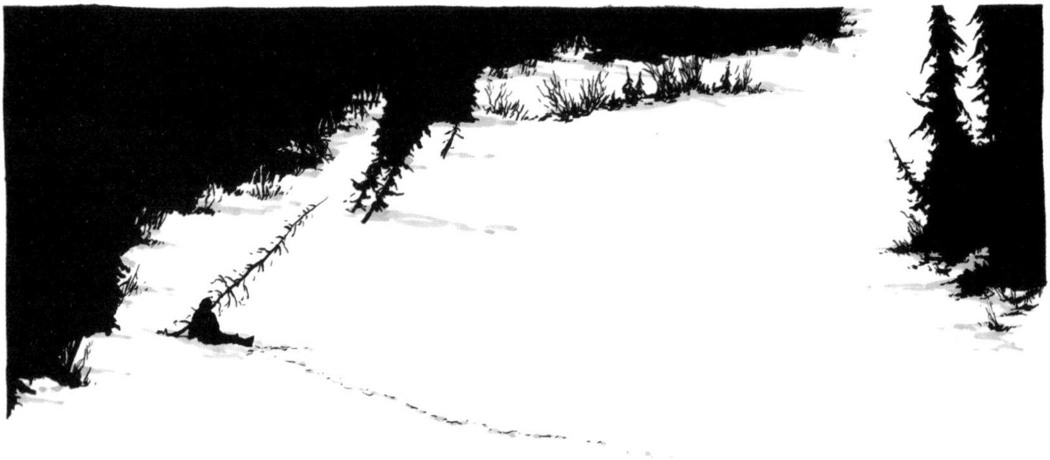